Steve Arnna
1-417-434-5508

# TALES FROM
# SAWYERTON
# SPRINGS

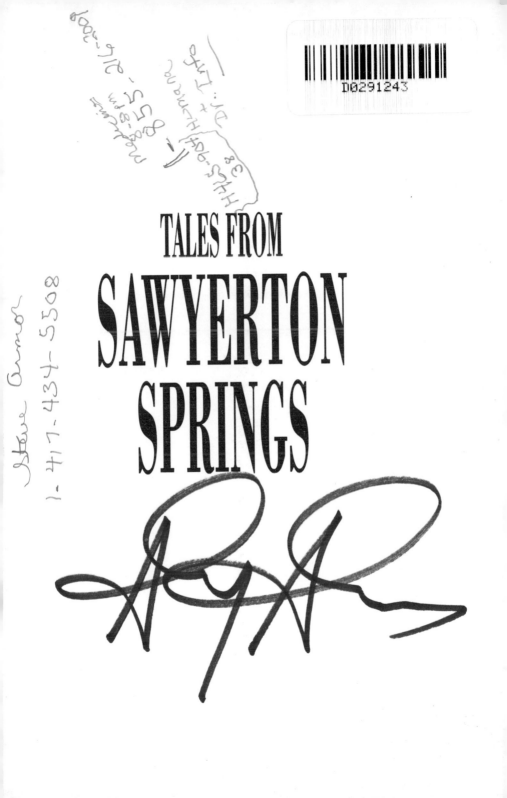

# TALES FROM
# SAWYERTON
# SPRINGS

*Andy Andrews*

Distributed to the trade by

PUBLISHERS
DISTRIBUTION SERVICE

Co-published by Country America Corporation
1716 Locust Street, Des Moines, IA 50309-3023

Danita Allen, Editor
Bill Eftink, Managing Editor
Ray Neubauer, Art Director
Dick Sowienski, Senior Editor
Grant Fairchild, Production Editor
and

LIGHTNING
CROWN
PUBLISHERS

P.O. Box 17321 Nashville,TN 37217
(800) 726-2639

Printed by Quebecor Printing Book Group
United States of America

FIRST EDITION
First Printing: May 1995
Library of Congress Catalog Card Number: 94-78252
ISBN: 0-9629620-4-X

Illustrations: Gregg Fitzhugh
Back Cover Photo: Denis Carney
Cover Design: Angela Saxon

# Contents

Acknowledgments

Introduction

Souped-Up Town ............................................................10

Baseball, Boys, and Bad Words ............................................18

Billy Pat's Midnight Adventure ...........................................28

Who Wants Socks? .........................................................36

Thigh Day at Doc's Open House ...........................................44

Don't Call Me Chicken! ...................................................52

Dad Had the Keys to the Kingdom .........................................60

The Grave Decision .......................................................66

Shootout in Sawyerton Springs ...........................................74

Crazy Hazey Forks Over the Head .........................................82

Ducking the Game Warden .................................................88

Wonderful Wheeler and the Flat-Out Lie ..................................96

Store Wars ..............................................................104

Mr. Michael Ted's Big Production .......................................112

The Secret War of Ginny Williams .......................................120

Billy Pat, Dick, and Gilligan, Too .....................................128

Unfair Tales of Midway Madness .........................................136

A Fowl Day Ends with Thanksgiving ......................................144

A Shining Light ........................................................152

Dying for a Valentine's Date ...........................................160

On the Bandwagon .......................................................168

The Treasure of the Oak ................................................176

Off the Road Again .....................................................184

You Reap What You Throw ................................................192

Monk's Back in Town ....................................................200

Dentist the Menace .....................................................206

Church Gangs and Other Hot Items .......................................214

## Dedication

To my wife, Polly, whose own memories of Sawyerton Springs
(by way of DeKalb, Mississippi) contributed greatly
to this book.

## Acknowledgments

Danita Allen, whose skill, patience, and encouragement have made this project possible.

Bill Eftink, who always sends those nice notes about my column being late (which is every month). Sorry, Bill.

Robert D. Smith, my manager and friend who grew up in a big city but is nice enough to have been from somewhere normal.

Isabel Galindo, Alejandra Galindo, and Sandie Dorff, who know more about my life than I do (where am I next week?).

Lucy, my Dalmatian, who keeps me company while I write.

The people of Sawyerton Springs (you know who you are!).

# Introduction

I first met Danita Allen, the editor of *Country America* magazine, on the *S.S. Norway*, a cruise ship sailing from Miami. After hearing me talk about growing up in a small town and an experience I had playing Little League baseball, she suggested that I write a story for the magazine. That first article, "Baseball, Boys, and Bad Words," received such an overwhelming response that we decided to run a second piece, which led to a third, and the rest, as they say, is history.

These accounts of my childhood in Sawyerton Springs soon expanded to include my friends who still live there. They are good people and quite tolerant, I believe, of the monthly invasion of privacy I now represent. They do, however, require that I tell the truth. Miss Edna Thigpen, being a journalist, is especially quick to call and point out any inaccuracies in my retelling of local events.

This brings me to the question I am most often asked, which is: "Where exactly is Sawyerton Springs?" Sorry, I just can't tell you. I can reveal its location to be in south Alabama, roughly triangulated between Dothan, Jackson, and Foley. If I were any more specific than that, the attention might create a tourist trap out of an area that did nothing to deserve it. And besides, Billy Pat Williams told me just the other day, "We aren't on any map yet, but if you publish one with those stories of yours—it's gonna be you and me!"

In any case, I do hope you enjoy this journey to a place most of us only visit in our memories. I am proud of Sawyerton Springs. It was a wonderful town in which to grow up . . . and a wonderful place to go back to now and again.

Andy Andrews
Gulf Shores, Alabama

Sawyerton Springs bought every single jar of chicken soup on that bus. Rick managed to put away two jars for Sue and himself in case they came down with the bug.

# Souped-Up Town

The flu epidemic that spread through Sawyerton Springs last month is now all but over. So, too, is the quiet gloating of those people who, for whatever reason, were lucky enough to escape the experience. Back in October, vaccinations had been offered free of charge by the county health department. Setting up shop in the fellowship hall of Beauman's Pond United Methodist Church, however, was not an overwhelming success.

People stayed away in droves. Most of the Baptists refused to participate in what they saw as "just another Methodist gimmick," and the Methodists didn't take advantage of the opportunity because of the nurse.

Miss Luna Myers, now in her eighty-third year, has been giving flu shots for the county since God was a boy. She looked like she was 100 years old back when she was working for Dr. Peyton. Lee Peyton, who got all his shots from Miss Luna as a kid and has now taken over his dad's practice, won't go near her. "She's so shaky," he says, "that there'll be five holes in your arm before she gets the medicine in. Every hole feels like it was made by a jackhammer!"

Needless to say, the line for Miss Luna's services last fall was a short one. And that, in a nutshell, seems to be why so many people have been sick. Oddly enough, however, Sawyerton Springs was the only town in the tri-county area where anyone so much as felt bad.

At the Williams house on Keating Drive, Billy Pat and Ginny are up and around again after two weeks of nausea, headaches, and what Billy Pat calls "The Big D." And it's a good thing, too, because Ginny had just about come to the end of her rope where Billy Pat was concerned. "Ginny, get me a glass of water. . . . Ginny, get me a blanket. . . . Ginny, let the dog out." *For goodness sake*, she thought, *doesn't he realize that I'm sick, too?*

"Shut up, Billy Pat. Get your own water!" That's what she wanted to say, but she didn't. Ginny felt it was her duty to be the strong one at times like these, so she poured his water and covered him with blankets—all the while feeling like the dog she was constantly letting in and out of the house.

Actually, most of the people in town feel like they might not have made it through this flu season if it hadn't been for Rick's Rolling Store. Rick's Rolling Store is really an old school bus from Birmingham that was put out to pasture in 1973. Rick Carper, who drove it for almost 15 years, said that if they were retiring his bus, then they could just, by gosh, retire him, too!

So Rick bought the bus and painted it red, white, and blue. He took out the seats and bolted shelves and racks all over the inside. After stocking the bus with every imaginable item, Rick and his wife, Sue, set out for Sawyerton Springs. It was their dream to somehow be of service to their fellow man. "And what better way to be of service," Rick said, "than to bring groceries to a hungry town."

Now, of course, there's Norman's Groceteria on College Avenue, but when Rick and Sue arrived with their bus 19 years ago, they were the only game in town. They sold soap, salt, pencils, vegetables, macaroni noodles, bolts of material, knives, candy, and even Sue's homemade pepper sauce. When you heard that big bus engine whine to a stop with those loud air brakes, all you had to do was go outside with your laundry basket, fill it with whatever you wanted, and your shopping was done for the week.

When Rick's Rolling Store first hit the streets, no one knew quite what to make of it . . . or why it was there in the first place. There seemed to be an abundance of theories. "They came from the city to spy on us," was the most popular choice, though no one could think of anything "the city" might want to know!

Actually, the reason that Rick and Sue chose Sawyerton Springs as the home base for Rick's Rolling Store was quite simple. First and foremost was the fact that everyone had to drive 20 minutes to a supermarket. But the sign on the edge of town clinched the deal.

In 1953, when the sign went up, the town council had a tremendous argument about what the town slogan should be. Every town, after all, had to have one. Several of the council members, acknowledging the fact that Dr. Peyton had just opened his office, were pushing for "Sawyerton Springs . . . Gateway to Medicine." They were voted down, as was the contingent that wanted "Sawyerton Springs . . . Speed Limit 25." What they settled on was "Sawyerton Springs . . . A Town You Will Like." That's the slogan that welcomed the Carpers years ago, and the same sign is still standing today.

The grand opening of Rick's Rolling Store is not likely to be forgotten. Rick somehow managed to run over two dogs and a cat the very first day. By the next week, another dog, another cat, and Bubba Pratt's right foot had all fallen victim to the store on wheels. "Thank God the man didn't open a Kmart," someone remarked, "he'd have wiped out the town!"

Before too long, Bubba, the animals, and the rest of the population had all gotten used to our town's new addition. As people became acclimated to shopping on a bus, Rick and Sue were gradually accepted and welcomed as friends. Rick was always quick with a joke and was generous with free candy for the kids while Sue enjoyed talking with the ladies wherever they stopped. Sue's pepper sauce had been such a hit that she frequently offered a monthly special of her homemade jam, bread, or anything else she produced in her spare time.

Nowadays, I suppose one could say that time has caught up with Rick's Rolling Store. What with Norman's Groceteria having a larger selection, people don't seem to be as inclined to buy from Rick and Sue. But they are a part of the town and you don't forget your own, so everyone still patronizes the bus occasionally. It's mostly little things like tape or a hairbrush, but people make the effort because they remember when the Carpers made an effort for them.

If Rick heard that Mrs. Perkins was looking for a camellia print pattern to make a special dress, he'd make a note, and the next week he'd have it.

Or if Sue found out that the Henleys liked bread 'n' butter pickles, that would be her homemade special of the month. Once, when Miss Luna Myers fell and broke her hip, they carried her, lying in the aisle of Rick's Rolling Store, all the way to the Foley Regional Medical Center—27 miles! People don't forget a thing like that.

When everyone fell ill last month, Rick and Sue were a godsend. Back and forth, all over town morning, noon, and night. Aspirin to the Rollins, four bottles of Pepto-Bismol for Billy Pat and Ginny, and juices for the Pratt children. The homemade chicken soup that Sue had made also continued to be a big seller, just as it had been when it first came out—a couple or three days before the town got sick.

As I mentioned earlier, most families buy their staples at Norman's and, as an unspoken gesture of appreciation, continue to buy and consume whatever Sue's Special happens to be that particular month. Near the end of January, Rick's Rolling store was stocked with Sue's chicken soup. She had made it with celery and carrots, a few mushrooms, and, of course, chicken. On the jars she had written in black Magic Marker, "salt and pepper to taste."

Within a week, well over half the soup was sold. It was obviously a good time of the year for that sort of thing, and despite the fact that it had a strange taste, most people ate what they had purchased and enjoyed it. It was about that time that Lee Peyton began seeing cases of the flu. It got pretty bad. Whole families were coming into his office together. "There's really nothing I can do," he told them. "Just go back to bed, and it'll run its course. One more thing," he added, "Eat some chicken soup—I hear Rick's Rolling Store has it this month."

And so they did. Sawyerton Springs bought every single jar of chicken soup on that bus. Rick managed to put away two jars for Sue and himself in case they came down with the bug, but other than that, they were sold out. "You know, honey," Rick said as Sue made the list for restocking, "This is the best month we've had since Norman opened up his place. I hate to take advantage of a bad situation, but your chicken soup is doing the trick for everybody!"

And it certainly looked that way. Within three or four days of a family's last jar, they were up and around. "Yessir," Bubba told Billy Pat over lunch last week, "it's a good thing we bought a case of that soup. We kept eating it and eating it until we ran out. Wasn't long after—we were okay."

"Same thing at our house," Billy Pat said.

Bubba continued, "We'd have never even thought about the soup if we hadn't eaten it the night we all got sick."

"Same thing at our house," Billy Pat said.

"My girls didn't want to eat it though . . . said it tasted weird. I told 'em, 'so what if it did. Eat it all,' I said, 'there's Chinese'd love to have it.' " Bubba paused, thinking. "Heck," he said, "that stuff did taste weird!"

"Same thing at our house," Billy Pat said, and they looked at each other. Suddenly, a wave of realization washed over them like the nausea had done a few days before. That soup was bad. No one had the flu. It was food poisoning!

As they checked around town, it was pretty much the same story with everybody. The Henleys, the Rollins, the Deas, even Lee Peyton's family all got deathly ill eating that chicken soup. The people who didn't eat the soup never got sick. The people who ate the soup, got sick, ate more soup, and stayed sick until the soup was gone.

I talked on the phone yesterday to several of the people who were affected, and a curious thing has happened. They've just decided not to say anything about it. "It's not as if they did it on purpose," Bubba said.

"No real harm was done," Glenda Perkins told me. "They're a part of our community, and were only trying to help."

Ginny Williams was concerned about Sue. "It'd kill her if she thought she'd hurt us."

So that's Sawyerton Springs. It's no wonder the town doesn't have a lawyer—they don't need one. No one has stopped buying the homemade specials from Rick's Rolling Store. The Carpers need the business. People have, however, stopped eating what they buy! But it's not a waste of money, and it's not viewed as dishonesty. It's just that Rick and Sue are important . . . and so are their feelings.

But the story doesn't end here. In fact, I believe there to be a sequel occurring as I write. Billy Pat and Bubba ran into Rick downtown this morning. "How's it going, Ricker?" Billy Pat asked, "Where's Sue?"

"Aw, she's visiting her sister in Birmingham," Rick replied, "so I'm being a bachelor."

"Want to come for supper?" Bubba asked. "Sandy and the kids would love to have you."

# Souped-Up Town

"No, but thanks anyway," Rick said, "I'm just going to stay home. It doesn't look like I'll catch that flu everybody else got, so I'm going to eat the last of our chicken soup. I never got any of it. Did you guys enjoy it?"

"Oh, yeah," Bubba said, "We ate it all."

And with a smile on his face, Billy Pat said, "Same thing at our house!"

We were literally on the ground. Coach
Simpson thought we were crying. He
sounded desperate as he tried to comfort
us, but the more he explained, the more
things got out of hand.

# Baseball, Boys, and Bad Words

Ꭵt was the first day of Little League practice. I was 11 years old, and this year I was going to be a "starter" at second base.

As we milled around, one could easily pick out the kids from last year's team: Lee Peyton, Kevin Perkins, Steve Krotzer, Phillip Inman, Charles Raymond Floyd, and, of course, me. We all had on last year's hats. They were off-white with a dark-blue bill and a big "FNB" on the front. First National Bank, our sponsor, would be giving everyone new hats. We knew that, but in the meantime, we wanted to be sure that our new coach could tell the veterans from the rookies.

None of us had met our new coach. His name was Mr. Simpson. He was, we were told, "new to the area." "New to the area" and "new in town" were two different things. If someone was "new in town," that generally meant that they had moved from someplace we had heard of and were probably still within driving distance of their cousins. "New to the area," however, was a hint that the person was "from the North." Living, as we did, in the southern part of Alabama, "North," to me, was Birmingham. At the time, I suppose I was somewhat suspicious of people from the North. This created an intense curiosity about Mr. Simpson. Almost a feeling of danger. After all, I had been told more than once that these people were nice, but different. The "but different" part was always said with a raised eyebrow.

Mr. Simpson parked his station wagon and gathered the equipment from the back. Bats, balls, helmets, catchers' gear. Yep, it was all there. We were watching from the backstop peering through the chicken wire as though he were some wild animal at the zoo. We noticed a boy with him. The boy had red hair and more freckles than I had seen on any human since my Aunt Nancy Jane (and she had freckles on her fingernails!). The boy, we figured, was the coach's son since Mr. Simpson also had red hair and more than his share of freckles.

"Hi, boys," Mr. Simpson said as he dumped the equipment near home plate. "My name is Hankin Simpson, and I'm your new coach."

I glanced to my right. Kevin Perkins was smirking and looking at me. Kevin was kind of a smart aleck, and I knew what he was thinking: *Hankin?*

Where did he come from?

Putting his hand on the shoulder of the red-headed boy, Mr. Simpson continued. "I want you to meet my son. This is Hankin, Jr."

I didn't dare look toward Kevin. I didn't need to. I could hear him smirking from where I was.

"Now, boys," the coach continued, "I'm new to the area."

*Well*, I thought, *that explains "Hankin."*

"But I'm sure," he said, "that it's going to be a great season. Okay? Okay! Now, before we begin practice, take a rap!" And with that, he clapped his hands and busied himself arranging the equipment.

# Baseball, Boys, and Bad Words

We shuffled our feet and looked at each other. *What*, we wondered, *did he want us to do? Take a what? A rap? What was a rap?*

Hankin, Jr., we saw, had begun to trot around the field, and, figuring that he knew what he was doing, we trotted after him.

"*Rap* is a Northern word," whispered Phillip as we jogged along. "It means 'to run'."

I wasn't sure whether to believe him or not. Kevin was a smart aleck, but Phillip Inman made things up. He was what 5 year olds called a storyteller, what we called a fibber, and what adults called a liar. He could look you right in the eye, tell you a fib, and he would be so convincing that you never doubted him. Even though I had never trusted him, I kept him as a friend because I had heard my dad tell my mom that he was sure to become president one day.

Back at home plate, all out of breath from running a rap, we gathered around Mr. Simpson, quite sure that he would now assign positions. We veterans thrust our caps toward his face, a virtual sea of FNBs, silently pleading with the man not to look at one of us and say, "Right field."

Since time began, all Little Leaguers have had a fear of right field. There are nine positions on a baseball diamond, and in the glamour department, right field ranks dead last. Most batters are right handed and hit the ball to left field; therefore, a coach who wants to avoid long losing streaks will naturally put his weakest player in "right."

I'd had my brush with this humiliation two years earlier as the weak link for Henley's Hardware Store (green hat; white "H"). Standing in right field game after game with nary a ball hit my way, I never believed the adults who told me I was an integral part of the team. I couldn't catch, but I wasn't stupid. A permanent residence in right field was an embarrassment. It was a curse. I was certain that I had been branded for the rest of my life. I could imagine myself as a grownup going to a job interview and being told, "I'm sorry, but there's just no place for you in the space program. I see on your record that you played right field."

"Boys," Mr. Simpson began, "we're going to be a winner this year. I'm excited about this team. Before we get started, I want to check you out at certain positions. Don't worry if you're new to the game. On my team, everyone gets to pray."

Excuse me? Did he say "pray"? I looked at Steve Krotzer. He was jabbing Charles Raymond Floyd in the ribs. Lee Peyton was jabbing Kevin and Phillip jabbed me.

"I know this is just practice," the coach continued, "but no matter, I want you to pray your hearts out!"

*This team*, I thought, *is in trouble*. Either someone had told our new leader that last year we lost 17 out of 23 games, or he took one look at us and decided that we were a bunch of rejects. What it boiled down to, I was beginning to believe, was that if we were to have a winning season, Mr. Simpson had settled on prayer as our only hope.

Thirty minutes later, we were in the positions that would be ours, more or less, for the rest of the year. I was at second base, so I was happy. Steve was at first; Kevin at third; Lee was our catcher; and Charles Raymond stood in right field with the other kids who couldn't catch.

Phillip Inman, meanwhile, pouted at shortstop. He wanted to pitch. Actually, we wanted him to pitch, too, but as soon as we had seen that there was a Hankin Simpson, Jr., we knew that he would not. Every member of "First National Bank" was acutely aware of that age-old Little League law: "If the coach has a son, the team has a pitcher."

This has become such an accepted part of coaching methodology that no one ever thinks to question it. A Little League coach is usually the father of one of the players, and he always has a blind spot where a son is concerned. Can the kid throw strikes? Has he got a curve ball? Does he trip over his own feet? It doesn't really matter, he's the coach's son. Put him on the mound and call him a pitcher.

# Baseball, Boys, and Bad Words

We practiced hard that first day. Trying to show Mr. Simpson our "stuff," we dove for grounders, swung for the fence, and generally showed as much hustle as we could muster. We didn't seem to be a vastly improved team from the year before. I blew a sure double play, our new pitcher was throwing the ball over the backstop, and Charles Raymond got hit in the head by a pop fly and cried.

Coach Simpson didn't say much, but when he did, he was still saying things we didn't understand: "Take another rap. Pray hard, pray hard!" We were a confused group of kids. It was at the end of practice, however, during the compulsory pep talk, when everything became crystal clear.

"There's one thing about this game you can count on," he said. "If you don't rearn to watch the basebarr hit the basebarr grove, you wirr never be an excerrent basebarr prayer!"

Well, we were stunned. After two and one-half hours of total darkness, we suddenly understood. A rap? Pray? He had wanted us to take a *lap*! He had wanted us to *play* hard! How could we not have figured it out?

From the depths of a pep talk to which no one was listening—like a bolt from the blue—those weird words all came together and made sense. Certain words from his last sentence jumped out at us like sparks from a bonfire. "Blah, blah, blah, rearn blah, blah, blah, basebarr, blah, blah, basebarr grove, blah, blah, wirr blah, blah, blah, excerrent basebarr prayer." It was now an undeniable fact that had become apparent to us all in one fell swoop. Coach Simpson could not say his *L*s!

We stood, silently exchanging furtive glances, as Hankin, Jr. and Sr., got in the car and drove away. No one had spoken a word yet, but we suspected that we had been the recipients of a miracle from God. We could scarcely contain our collective excitement. To a group of 11-year-old boys, nothing beats having a human target at which to laugh. Double the fun if the boys are able to mimic the target, and triple if the unfortunate target happens to be an adult!

Kevin was smirking again. We shuffled around and snickered a few minutes. Then it started.

Charles Raymond: "I'm a basebarr prayer [laughter]."

Steve: "No, you ain't. You're a right fierder [laughter]!"

Kevin: "Take a rap! Take a rap [hard laughter]!"

Lee: "Coach Simpson? I rike him. I rearry do [convulsions]!"

Phillip: "My name is Phirrip [on the ground rolling]!"

Kevin: "Take a rap! Take a rap [red faces, stomach aches, no oxygen]!"

And so it continued until we were exhausted. Finally, able to breathe at last, we lounged in the dirt around home plate. Phillip spoke first. "I think he's Oriental," he said. "Oriental people use the letter R in place of the letter L when they speak English because they don't have the letter L in their own language. That's why he does it. Coach Simpson is Oriental. Remember? He said he was new to the area. He's Oriental."

"Oriental?" Charles Raymond asked. "Isn't that when you know your way around?"

Kevin smirked. "No, Stupe," he said. "He means Japanese. Right?"

Kevin glanced my way. I wanted to tell Phillip that I had never seen a 6-foot-3-inch, 240-pound, red-haired, freckled-faced Japanese guy before. That's what I wanted to say, but Phillip was looking at me with such an air of self-confidence that I knew the truth did not have a chance against such a convincing opponent.

I was about to give it a try anyway when Lee suddenly giggled.

"What?" we demanded.

"I was just thinking," Lee said as he tried to talk through his laughter. "I was just thinking that one day this year I'm gonna be rounding third."

He stopped and laughed. "I'm gonna be rounding third headed toward this here home plate and . . ." He was really laughing now.

"Tell us!" we said.

# Baseball, Boys, and Bad Words

"I'm gonna be headed toward this here home plate, and Coach Simpson's gonna yell, 'Sride, Ree, sride!' "

That did it. We were off and running again.

We never mentioned the Oriental theory again. Kevin told me privately one day that he thought Phillip was "full of mess." I took that to be Kevin's way of saying that he didn't believe Coach Simpson was Japanese either. Not that it would have mattered. One of our best friends, Peter Chin, was Japanese or something. He said his Ls perfectly, too, except, of course, when he was mimicking Coach Simpson with us!

Several memories of that year still remain clear in my mind. To this day, Philip Inman is "Phirrip" to everyone who played on that team. And no one has forgotten the game that Lee Peyton rounded third, headed for home, and fell down before he got there, laughing, because Coach Simpson really did yell, "Sride, Ree, sride!"

If I had to choose one capsule of time during that season to carry with me for the rest of my life, it would have to be the day Steve Krotzer got kicked off the team. Maybe "kicked off" is too harsh. Actually, he was transferred to another team because the league president found that Steve's family was living in another district.

It was a messy situation. Steve had played with us for four years. Two years on Henley's Hardware Store and two with First National Bank. Now they were sending him to play with the team—Cabell's Gas Station—near his home. We were sick. Steve was our friend and a darn good first baseman. He didn't want to go. We didn't want him to leave. But that last day did arrive.

When practice was over, Coach Simpson gathered us around the pitcher's mound. He had his hand on Steve's shoulder. "Boys," he said, "this is a sad day. We're going to miss Steve. He's a fine barr prayer and a fine young man."

Steve was close to tears. We were, too.

"I don't understand the inner workings of the system," Coach Simpson continued, "and I'm not sure why this has happened. But I do know one thing . . . and rook at me when I say this because this is important. I want everyone of you to know that this was not Steve's faurt."

As a group, Steve included, we jumped as if ten thousand volts of electricity had passed through our bodies. Did he say what we thought he said? Surely not.

"No," he continued, "this was not Steve's faurt and it wasn't my faurt."

Yes, he did most definitely absolutely, too, say what we thought he said!

Oh, sure, we knew what he meant; we'd been unconsciously translating Simpsonisms all year. He was telling us that it wasn't Steve's "fault," but that wasn't what we were hearing!

"It wasn't Steve's parent's faurt either. I guess it was nobody's faurt," he said.

It was too good to be true. Of all the words in the world guaranteed to make 11-year-old boys laugh, only one of them is all by itself at the top of the list. And our coach, an adult, was saying that word over and over. And over.

"If it's anyone's faurt, it's the system's faurt. So don't pin the faurt on any one person, because it is just not their faurt!"

Well, I am not exaggerating when I say that we were literally laying on the ground. We were crying! Coach Simpson thought we really were crying and became concerned. He sounded desperate as he tried to comfort us, but the more he explained that it wasn't our "faurt" the more out of hand things became. Soon, tears were rolling down Coach Simpson's face, too. Several of us felt badly about that later, but, as Kevin said, "Hey, don't worry about it. It ain't our faurt!"

I haven't seen Coach Simpson in years. Kevin Perkins and Steve Krotzer were in my wedding. Lee Peyton went to medical school and returned to practice in our town. Charles Raymond

Floyd, our right fielder, was a late bloomer. He was a center fielder in college, made second-team All American, and played three years of minor league ball. I've totally lost track of Phillip Inman. The last I heard, he was a used car salesman and mayor of a small town in Louisiana.

I still remember us all as we were that summer. I can close my eyes and hear the explosions of laughter as we reacted to something that was, to us, the funniest thing in the world. And I feel a little sad when I think that when we were 11 years old, we may have laughed harder than we ever would again.

*Turning to walk back to his house, Billy Pat froze. Headlights. And they were coming right at him.*

# Billy Pat's Midnight Adventure

For several hours last week, the whole town was buzzing. It didn't matter where I went, everyone was talking about the same thing. "Did you hear," they would say, "about Billy Pat Williams' midnight walk?" I had indeed, and, in fact, seeing as how it was now close to noon in our small town, who hadn't? Actually, Billy Pat's walk did not occur at midnight. It took place somewhere around 2 a.m., but I'm getting ahead of myself.

Billy Pat Williams has lived in Sawyerton Springs for 19 years, which is not enough time to be considered anything more than a newcomer by some of our older citizens. It is of no significance to some of them that he once served two terms on the county commission or that he and his wife, Ginny, raised three daughters here. Most of them (at least silently) agree with the outspoken

29

opinion of Miss Luna Myers, who once told her Golden Agers Sunday School class, "If you weren't born here, get out."

Another strike against him is his occupation. Billy Pat owns and operates the only Toyota dealership in the tri-county area. One must understand that this in itself verges on original sin among townspeople who drive Fords and Chevrolets almost without exception. Why, you might ask, would someone drive the same kind of car for 30 years? "Because my father did," is the answer, "and his before him. And if you want to drive a foreign car, get out."

It isn't my intention to portray these people as rude or unkind. In fact, quite the opposite is true. There is, however, a set of standards by which one is expected to abide in a small town, and if you don't, well, Birmingham is only a few hours away!

Everyone likes Billy Pat, though. It's obvious in the way he is treated. He is talked about, laughed at, and watched very darn carefully for any wrong move. Remember, this is a small town, if he wasn't liked, he'd just be ignored.

Billy Pat, Ginny, and their three daughters have lived in their present home on Keating Drive for four years now. It's the only two story, red-brick, three-bedroom, two-and-one-half bathroom house in the neighborhood. That in itself would have been enough for a week's worth of gossip, but Billy Pat and Ginny didn't just move in to an existing house. They built it.

For weeks and weeks and weeks it went on. "So, Billy Pat, I see over on Keating Drive where a wood house ain't good enough for ya." Or "Well, well. Here comes Billy Pat. Maybe we should call you Mr. Billy Pat now that you're building that mansion over on Keating." Rick Carper, who lives down the street, got in the best one. "Say Billy Pat," he said, "what's a half a bathroom? Is that for when you've only got to go a little bit?"

And on it went. Recently, after a five-car month at the dealership, Billy Pat considered putting in a pool, but Ginny wouldn't let him do it. "No need to throw our good fortune in someone else's face," she said. Besides, she was close friends with Rebecca Peyton, Lee's wife, and she knew that when they built their pool and had that beautiful fountain installed, they never got to use it. Every night, someone would throw a box of laundry detergent over the fence, into the water, and what with that fountain . . . well, she was not going to go through that!

The three girls, Bonnie Pat, Janine, and Janelle, are a source of pride for their parents. They're relatively nice looking, have never made below a C on any report card ever, and most importantly, they don't drink. Billy Pat, however, will admit, if pressed, that Janelle has come in on more than one Friday night acting kind of goofy.

When Billy Pat feels the need to escape the female environment in which he lives, he'll slip out the back door, whistle for his dog, Barney, and take a walk. Up Keating toward Cherokee, on Cherokee for a bit, a right on Randal, and then they cut through the Rollins' backyard back to Keating and home.

Billy Pat loves these times with Barney. Barney never talks back, never asks him to fix anything, never asks "why." I ran into them yesterday evening, and as we exchanged pleasantries, I patted Barney's black and white spotted head. "Watch out," Billy Pat warned, "if he bites you, you'll be doomed to eternal Dalmatian!" We both chuckled. It didn't matter that Billy Pat says that every time I pet his dog. He's a nice guy, so I laugh. I didn't, however, mention his midnight walk. I wasn't sure he'd want to talk about it. I'd already heard the story from eight people anyway.

As I understand it, Barney was a gift. Not a gift to Billy Pat, but a gift from him. Billy Pat bought the dog from a breeder in Birmingham, and he fully intended to give him as a birthday present to Dick Rollins, his best friend. Dick's birthday was still three days away, so Billy Pat had decided to let his family enjoy the pup in the meantime.

Why, he wondered as he drove home with that cute puppy in his lap, did a man feel some primal urge to give an animal as a present to another man? It was almost as weird as Ginny's compulsion to fix up her unmarried friends with blind dates! But there he was, heading home with a dog he couldn't give to Dick until Tuesday.

When Billy Pat opened the sliding glass door to the den and put the puppy on the floor, the reaction he observed in Ginny and the girls led him to believe he might have made a mistake. And he had. The pup looked at him slyly as if to say, "Gotcha! You didn't really think you could keep me for a while and then give me away, did you?" And sure enough, after three days, Dick Rollins received a case of shotgun shells, and Barney was Billy Pat's dog.

Last Wednesday night, Billy Pat and Ginny crawled into bed about 10:30. They were both exhausted. Ginny had spent what felt like a year that day cleaning the house, and Billy Pat was emotionally drained. Serving as chairman of the Grace Fellowship Baptist Church Planning Committee did that to him. Earlier that evening, after prayer meeting, he had spent a good solid hour listening to Roger Luker and Miss Luna Myers debate the pros and cons of a covered dish social versus catering by Bubba's Fried Chicken.

They went to sleep quickly, despite a disagreement over whose night it was to shut off the bathroom light. (Billy Pat's it turned out.) Everything was quiet until sometime after midnight when Billy Pat was jolted awake by a blood-curdling scream and the words, "Help! They're killing him!"

Billy Pat rolled onto the floor carrying the sheets and bedspread with him. He was halfway under the bed when he came fully awake. In the momentary fog, he hadn't been certain whether or not he was the one being killed! Suddenly, he realized that it was Ginny who was screaming, and as he scrambled to untangle himself from the possibility of death by linen, he heard Bonnie Pat, Janine, and Janelle join in the chorus.

Only a few minutes before, Ginny had sleepily gone to the bathroom for a glass of water. Returning to her side of the bed, she paused at the front window and glanced down the street. Noticing movement under the street light, Ginny stared intently and immediately made sense of the motion. It was a dogfight . . . and right in the middle of it was Barney!

By the time Billy Pat made it off the floor and to the window, the three girls were crying and screaming as loud as their mother, who, by now, was also yelling at Billy Pat. "For heaven's sake, Billy Pat," she shrieked, "do something!"

And so he did. He ran to the front door and bolted outside. Showing an amazing presence of mind usually reserved for veterans of combat or big city paramedics, Billy Pat knew he could not break up the dogfight with his bare hands. On his way off the porch, he grabbed the American flag that always hung from the railing on an eight-foot pole and ran down the street as fast as he could go.

Arriving at the scene of the dogfight, he held the flagpole high over his head and swept the flag into the pack—back and forth. Billy Pat threw a schnauzer into a neighbor's yard. A collie-shepherd mix was knocked off his feet, dogs were flying everywhere. He even hit Barney on the back. The look of surprise on the dogs' faces was evident. It was as if they were saying, "Is that your dad, Barn? What's he doing out here in the middle of the night?"

Though it seemed to Billy Pat that an enormous amount of time had passed, within 30 seconds of joining the hostilities, he stood alone. The dogs, either from a fear of the flagpole or a belief that the bearer of it was insane, had all disappeared. He listened and could hear nothing but his own heavy breathing.

Turning to walk back to his house, Billy Pat froze. Headlights. And they were coming right at him. It was as if Billy Pat Williams woke up again in just that instant, because he had a clear mental image of exactly how he looked: an upstanding member of the community, who just happened to be wearing red satin boxer shorts and carrying an American flag down the middle of the street at two o'clock in the morning!

As Billy Pat stood there, bathed in the approaching light, he couldn't even come up with a plausible lie about exactly what in the world he was doing. Before he even thought to run, the car pulled up. Naturally, it was Jeff Deas, the town's only policeman. For a moment, neither said a word. Then, shining his flashlight from the red satin boxers to Billy Pat's face, Jeff cocked an eyebrow and said simply, "Billy Pat?"

"I know you're wondering what I'm doing out here," Billy Pat replied. "I'm breaking up dogfights."

They looked around. Not a dog in sight.

"Billy Pat," Jeff said with a smirk on his face, "you're doing a wonderful job."

As Billy Pat watched the tail lights of the patrol car vanish down the street, he knew he had not heard the last of this. And he hasn't. He won't hear the last of it for a very long time. But he doesn't really mind. He thinks it's pretty funny himself, and, after all, he lives in a small town—if they didn't like him, nobody would've said a word.

Who wanted socks? What kind of
Christmas present was that? I had
socks—a whole drawer full of them.

# Who Wants Socks?

T here are 24 hours in a day. Only 24. That translates to 1,440 minutes or 86,400 seconds. Every single day of my adult life.

But as a boy, there was one night every year that lasted longer than any other—one night when clocks actually slowed down. This phenomena generally occurred near the end of December, specifically on the night of the 24th . . . Christmas Eve.

I had gone to bed at 9:00 p.m. after leaving a note, pound cake, and a glass of buttermilk for Santa Claus. Every Christmas Eve for as many of my seven years as I could remember, that's what I left him: a note, pound cake, and a glass of buttermilk.

The note contained the usual niceties about being careful not to slip on the roof and saying hello to Rudolph, but its primary purpose was, of course, to make one last stab at getting the presents I wanted! The pound cake was left over from Jesus' birthday party, which we had celebrated before bedtime, and the buttermilk . . . well, the buttermilk was always left because my dad insisted that it was Santa's favorite drink. Personally, I hated the stuff, but since my father drank it by the gallon, I assumed he knew!

By 10:30, I was still awake. I was mentally tracing Santa's route to our house at 1505 Randal Road. It did concern me somewhat that he might not find me because of a mistake on the road signs. Randal at one end of our road was spelled with one L, and at the other end, the sign proclaimed Randall (two Ls).

Would he be able to locate me? Maybe he would get confused, come in from Randal Road once, and later enter the neighborhood by way of Randall Road, and I'd get presents twice. Not likely, I knew, but these are the kinds of things a kid thinks about on Christmas Eve!

Earlier, I had heard on the local news that Santa's sleigh had been tracked on radar leaving Thailand, and the predictions were that he would soon be in Singapore. I wasn't sure where Singapore was, but I thought it might be near Mississippi, which was the state next to us. In any case, that's why I went to bed at 9:00!

11:00. I wasn't even sleepy! I could smell the Christmas tree from the bedroom. My dad loved Christmas and would have had our tree up, trimmed, and glowing by Labor Day if my mom had let him, but as she told him every year, our family was not going to skip Thanksgiving.

As it was, the tree had been decorated since the day after Thanksgiving and would remain so until a loud discussion occurred between my parents. This discussion usually took place around the first of February. Although my mother consistently prevailed and the tree did come down, I always thought my dad had a strong argument by pointing out that just because the needles had fallen off the tree, that didn't necessarily mean it was dead!

The tree itself stretched 50 feet into the air. The fact that we only had an eight foot ceiling casts a shadow of doubt on my recollection of this particular point, but you get the idea—it was a big tree!

We bought a blue spruce every year. That variety was, according to my dad, the only *real* Christmas tree. A blue spruce was more aromatic and, he explained, wouldn't get sap all over the

# Who Wants Socks?

carpet like "a stinkin' Scotch pine!"

Family tradition dictated that we had to make our own decorations. Though the tree looked beautiful to me, in actuality, it was probably kind of junky. Construction paper chains, stars shaped out of pipe cleaners, and bells made from foil-covered Dixie Cups were everywhere. I hung a toilet brush from the bathroom on it one year, and no one noticed for days!

At 12:01 a.m. it was technically Christmas, but I knew better than to venture into the living room. I was to stay in bed until Mom and Dad came to get me—and besides, I didn't want to blow the whole deal. I had been warned repeatedly that Santa would not come until I was asleep.

But how was I supposed to sleep? This was only the most incredible day of the year. There was no way I could go to sleep! I'd have to fake it and just hope Santa wasn't as sharp as everyone said. No way was I going to sleep. I just wouldn't! Heck, I'd already been awake for a week. I'd just stick it out 'til daylight.

"Son? Son!" My father shook me. I opened my eyes, and he said, "Santa has been here!"

Ignoring the fact that I had indeed gone to sleep, I jumped out of bed and ran to the living room. The tree (more than 100 feet tall now) was almost covered with gifts and toys of every sort. There was the basketball I'd asked for! Where was the BB gun? There was the Incredible Edible Machine—now I could make bugs to eat in front of my sister! Where was my BB gun? Ah, my Candyland game! Baseball glove! G.I. Joe! My BB gun must be one of the wrapped presents!

But it wasn't. Neither was the electric football game I'd wanted. I did, however, get two sweaters, blue jeans, a white belt, and from my Aunt Nancy Jane . . . socks.

Socks. Who wanted socks? What kind of Christmas present was socks? I had socks. I had a whole drawer full of socks. I was not pleased!

All in all, however, my haul was impressive. I had scored on some of the main things I'd wanted, and if I didn't think about the clothes and especially the socks—I was happy.

Before too long, the most important part of Christmas was at hand. My dad was asleep in his recliner, Mom was in the kitchen, and I was now free to compare loot with my friends.

This ritual, practiced by every kid since time began, was a large part of our growing up process. Seven years old seems a little early to be concerned with "keeping up with the Joneses," but that's exactly what we did.

My first stop was two houses down. Wayne Gardner had gotten a bicycle. It had a tiger-striped banana seat and spider handlebars. It was beautiful, but he wouldn't let me ride it so I left. Later that day, while showing off for Kathy Barr, Wayne tried to pop a wheelie, fell off the bike, and cried. I laughed.

Down the street, Mike and Jody Rawls were in the guinea pig business. Mr. Rawls had made a trip to the emergency room early that morning after being bitten by the one named Charley. He hated those guinea pigs after that, but he never again tried to put a bow on one!

Roger Luker had gotten the electric football game I had wanted. Graciously pointing out the flaws in that particular model, I generally acted unimpressed. Roger had also received the Rock 'Em Sock 'Em Robots. We didn't play with them because, thanks to his brother Stephen, they were already broken.

Lee Peyton's dad was a doctor. They lived across Cherokee Avenue in another, much nicer neighborhood. I hated going to Lee's house that morning. I knew what Lee had gotten for Christmas—everything! He had an Operation game, Battleship, a tetherball set, the deluxe model electric football game, a real minibike (four horsepower), a bicycle like Wayne's, only better, a trampoline, a swing set, and a BB gun!

I stayed at Lee's house for more than an hour. Lee really knew how to show a kid a good time. We dug a hole in the vacant lot

# Who Wants Socks?

next door and put the box from the trampoline over it. Great fort!

Walking home, I was imagining Christmas dinner. I felt sure that we'd have the same wonderful menu that we'd had the year before: turkey and dressing with cranberry sauce, sweet potato casserole with pecans on the top, peas, corn, pickled peaches, and homemade rolls. I walked faster.

Rounding the corner behind the Vine and Olive Hotel, I saw Timmy Johnson and his sister, Barbara, tossing an old tennis ball in their front yard. As usual, neither was wearing a jacket, though the temperature was in the forties. Timmy was in my class at school; Barbara was three years older.

They didn't seem to have many friends. Even at lunchtime they would go out on the playground to swing from the Jungle Gym or just talk. They never went with us into the cafeteria and never brought a sack lunch. The Luker boys said it was because they were snobs. I thought maybe so, too.

"Hi, Timmy," I said as I approached. "What'd you get for Christmas? I got everything I wanted except a BB gun and an electric football game!"

They continued tossing the ball. Back and forth. Thinking he didn't hear me, I tried again. "Hey! Show me what you got for Christmas!"

Never looking at me, Timmy mumbled, "I got these shoes."

I could see the shoes he had received. Big, black, hard-leather shoes that looked as if they might belong to my grandfather. But they were shined, polished, and tied directly onto his feet. Barbara had on a pair that didn't appear to be drastically different.

I had never seen either of them with anything other than tennis shoes. Once, Timmy was sent home from school for showing up barefooted. After that, he was absent for a week.

Watching them continue to throw the ball, I noticed something not quite right. I said, "That's not the way you're supposed to wear those shoes."

The ball fell to the ground. As they turned to face me, Barbara said, "What do you mean by that? We're wearing them just like you are—on our feet!"

She looked mad. I tried to explain myself. "Yeah, that's right," I stammered, "but you're not wearing socks. You're supposed to wear socks with those kind of shoes."

For a moment we stared at each other. Then, without warning, Timmy started crying and ran inside. Barbara called me a name and ran after him. I stood there a few minutes wondering what I had done. I even knocked on their door, but no one answered, so I went home.

When I arrived, I told my parents what had happened with Timmy and Barbara. I told them exactly what I'd said. My mom had tears running down her cheeks as my dad picked me up and carried me to my bedroom. I thought I was about to get a spanking, but instead, he hugged me.

He told me all about why Lee Peyton got big presents and why I didn't get an electric football game. Gently, he explained to me about Santa Claus and buttermilk. And then, wiping the tears from my face, he told me why my friends didn't wear socks with their shoes.

I now remember that day as an awakening. I had never known there were families without enough to eat. Amid all the decorations and songs and parties surrounding our most magical holiday, it had never occurred to me that some parents might do without the luxury of socks for their children simply because they couldn't afford them.

Many holiday seasons have passed since that year. Timmy and Barbara moved away while I was in the fourth grade, and I never saw them again, but I have never forgotten that Christmas. Wherever I live, there will always be people in my own neighborhood who are, in some way, less fortunate than I. And to this day, there is one Christmas gift I treasure above all others—the gift of a pair of socks.

*Miss Edna provides Sawyerton Springs
with something to talk about—usually,
the mistakes found in that week's edition.*

# Thigh Day at Doc's Open House

"Two ninety-five for a bucket of thighs—you can't even cook 'em at home that cheap—and I didn't get any!" That's what Ginny Williams told me over the phone last night when I called to ask about the success of "Thigh Day" at Bubba's Fried Chicken.

More than likely, it would have never come to my attention had I not read about it on page two of last week's *Sawyerton Springs Sentinel*, "The State's Eighth Oldest Newspaper." There was a big picture of Bubba, his wife, Sandy, and their four kids in front of the restaurant. Behind them, over the door, stretched a big banner that proclaimed: WE ARE OVERSTOCKED!

I suppose Thigh Day might not have been reported in most towns. Certainly the majority of newspapers would have overlooked the event, but Miss Edna Thigpen, the editor of the state's eighth oldest newspaper feels an obligation to her readers. Until recently, when she discovered that she was running the state's eighth oldest newspaper, the *Sentinel's* official motto had been "All the News." That is still her goal.

Even though I left Sawyerton Springs years ago, I still subscribe to the *Sentinel*. It only costs nine dollars a year, and it allows me to share in the daily occurrences of the town in which I grew up.

How else would I know that the Genealogical Society had held its meeting last week at Tucker Brollier's house? According to the *Sentinel*, Mr. Brollier was a wonderful host, serving members and guests punch and pound cake from a beautifully decorated table.

Mr. Brollier, a native of Dothan, now residing in Sawyerton Springs, also presented the program, which was a detailed account of the history of the house, known locally as the Constance Foley residence. A good time was had by all.

The article went on to compliment Mr. Brollier on restoring the flower beds "of which Constance was so proud" and listed the names of all the members who, incidentally, answered the roll call by naming "favorite women in the Bible." Next month's program, I understand, will be presented by Sue Carper, who will speak on "What Happened to the Confederate Dead at Gettysburg."

The *Sentinel* has been owned and operated by Miss Edna since she took over from her father in 1948. She is pretty much the bottom line where editorial content is concerned. In fact, the only part of the paper she doesn't control is the weekly column, "What's On My Mind," written by her best friend and roommate, Miss Luna Myers.

Miss Edna and Miss Luna have lived together since they both turned 60, and it became apparent that neither would ever marry. Both are tall, thin, and have short, jet-black hair, which, at a glance, is quite obviously dyed. They are both 83 years old and, despite their age, show no signs of slowing down.

Miss Luna, in addition to her weekly column and occasional duties as a reporter, still works with the county health department and chairs several committees at the Grace Fellowship Baptist Church. Miss Edna, however, is a different story. The newspaper is her life. She writes the articles, takes the pictures, and sells the advertising. On Thursday evenings, she even stands over the boys from the high school shop class as they run her ancient printing press.

The *Sentinel* hits the streets early Friday morning and has usually been read by everyone in town by lunch. Week after week, Miss Edna provides Sawyerton Springs with something to talk about. Usually, what they talk about are the mistakes they found in that week's edition.

No one really minds. "After all, she's 83," they'll say. "It's just a blessing she's still with us!"

Finding the mistakes has become a pastime for most of the townsfolk. Rather than mentioning the errors directly (that would be disrespectful to Miss Edna), most people simply slide them into their conversation. For instance, Billy Pat Williams might say to Jeff Deas' son, "Hey, Devin! Great game the other night. I saw in the paper where you scored two *touchdogs*!" They'd both smile and go on their way.

Last December, the Christmas edition came out with PEACE OF EARTH! printed on the front page. Shortly thereafter, the sign on Roger Luker's real estate office read: THE PRICES WILL NEVER BE BETTER—GET YOUR PIECE OF EARTH NOW! The spelling was different, but everyone knew what he meant.

Miss Edna, in my estimation, also has a history of being overly dramatic in her choice of words. When I was 14, I was one of several boys caught rolling the yard of a teacher. We had gotten together one night and decided that Mrs. Green, of sixth period English, needed toilet paper in her yard. And in her trees. And on her house.

Suffice it to say, we did a wonderful job, but we got caught and were forced by our parents, our principal, and Mrs. Green's husband, Jim, to clean up the mess. The next day, a picture of us doing so appeared on the *Sentinel's* front page—along with a caption that read VANDALS ARRESTED AND PUNISHED!

This past week, however, Miss Edna finally took the cake. And if you wondered why Ginny Williams missed out on the thighs at Bubba's Fried Chicken, here is your answer.

It all started when Dr. Lee Peyton decided to have a small party at his office on Friday evening. It was to be a celebration of two years in family practice, and only the people who owned businesses in town were asked to attend. The invitations, which were done in Old English script, stated simply: "You are cordially invited to attend an open house at the office of Dr. Lee Peyton between the hours of 5:30 p.m. and 8:00 p.m., Friday, the sixteenth of this month. Food and drink will be served."

All 24 invitations were mailed early in the week. No RSVP had been requested—it was just assumed that everyone would show up. That's kind of how things work in Sawyerton Springs. If you're asked to be somewhere, you go. It doesn't matter if it's a party or to help a neighbor fix a leaky septic tank. Of course, it's always more fun if it's a party.

On Thursday, Lee and his wife, Rebecca, spent the afternoon readying the office. It wasn't so much that Rebecca wanted to decorate; she just wanted certain things out of sight. "For gosh sakes, Lee," she said as she rolled her eyes, "people will be eating and drinking. They don't want to be staring at an exhibit of what happens to an ear when you don't wash it!"

Down, also, came the "Smoker's Lung" poster and the photographic enlargement of an ingrown toenail. Together they moved an examining table into the lobby. Lee began to cover it with a sheet, but one look from Rebecca told him he'd better get the tablecloth from home like she'd told him earlier.

The menu was set—pimento cheese sandwiches cut into small triangles, chicken salad sandwiches cut into small squares, and tuna fish on rye sandwiches cut into fingers. Mixed nuts, apple tarts, and vanilla wafers were also to be served. Rebecca had

# Thigh Day at Doc's Open House

already made the sandwiches and stored them in the refrigerator. The nuts, tarts, and wafers, along with Cokes and coffee were to be picked up from Norman's Groceteria around 3:00 the next day.

Friday morning, Lee and Rebecca slept late. This being Lee's normal day off, the clinic wasn't open, and what with the party later that afternoon, they figured to need the rest. In any case, neither of them left the house until it was time to go by Norman's. So neither of them saw the *Sentinel*.

It wasn't until about ten minutes after 5:00 when Lee strolled outside the office. "I'm going to make sure the yard is clean," he said to his wife as the door shut behind him. Actually, he knew the yard was clean, but darn it, she was making him nervous. "Watch where you sit. Don't touch the apple tarts!"

*Geez, Louise*, he thought as he picked the paper out of the azalea bushes, *this is just a little get-together. It's not like we're having the whole town for supper!* Lee chuckled as he broke the rubber band and opened the *Sentinel*.

Suddenly, his face went white. There, on the front page, above the fold, was the invitation to the open house. His jaw dropped to his knees as he tried to comprehend what he was seeing. Evidently, Miss Edna Thigpen of the *Sawyerton Springs Sentinel*, "The State's Eighth Oldest Newspaper," believing that everyone else got an invitation, too, reprinted it verbatim. She even included a story about proper dress on such an occasion!

"Geez, Louise," Lee said as he dropped the paper and bolted for the door, "we're having the whole town for supper . . . and they're all going to be here in about 5 minutes!"

Actually, it took about 30 minutes for the town to get there, but the food was gone in 5! About 400 people actually showed up, and all of them were hungry. Lee had already given Rebecca a sedative and was about to take one himself when he had an idea.

*Bubba. Yes, that might do it*, he thought. Bubba Pratt had told him yesterday that he and Sandy would be late to the party because he would be frying thighs. Anticipating an early rush the next morning, Bubba was cooking in advance!

And so with one phone call, Thigh Day was cancelled and the party was saved. And no one beyond Lee and Rebecca or Bubba and Sandy ever knew there was a problem . . . or who created it!

As for Miss Edna, she was never told what happened. Despite the fact that she reviewed the party and made derogatory comments about serving the dark meat of a chicken, neither Lee or Rebecca ever said a word. Bubba never got rattled or upset. In fact, none of them seemed to mind the trouble Miss Edna had caused.

"After all, she's 83," they said, "it's just a blessing she's still with us!"

*The weight and angle of the rope had pulled me (screaming) from the relative safety of the board platform.*

# Don't Call Me Chicken!

**M**y heart was pounding. For several minutes, I hadn't moved, and my friends were becoming impatient. "C'mon already—go!" Kevin Perkins yelled at me. He and Jeff Deas were standing at the base of the oak in which I was precariously perched. With my left hand, I held a branch of the big tree, while my right was wrapped in a death grip around "the rope."

"The rope" was well known in Sawyerton Springs. It was tied to a sturdy limb almost ninety feet up in the old General's Oak, which stood on the banks of Beauman's Pond. Some of the older boys had climbed the tree several years before and, after securing the rope, also nailed a board onto one of the back branches. As they stood on the board, which was at least 40 feet from the ground, they knotted and cut the rope to specifications.

Unfortunately, the specifications accommodated kids three or four years older and quite a few inches taller than the kids my age. An average size teenager could comfortably stand on the board, grasp the rope with both hands, and leisurely swing out over the water before splashing down.

My first swing attempt had been only three weeks earlier when, because of my size, I hadn't quite been able to obtain the proper grip with both hands. Of course, this fact did not become clear to me until I was prematurely propelled into midair.

The weight and angle of the rope had pulled me (screaming) from the relative safety of the board platform. Desperately, I had scrambled to hold on as I bounced over each knot on the speeding rope, finally catching the last knot under my arm as I reached the edge of the water. Lacking the strength to hold on, my body sailed through a wild pyracantha bush and into the pond. My nose was bloody. I was bruised and scratched from head to toe—but, I was alive!

Now, as I stood frozen, that memory came flooding back to haunt me. I let go of the rope and turned to climb from the tree. Suddenly, a single word from my friends below, spoken loudly and in unison, snapped me back to reality.

"Chicken!"

Well, there it was. I might have known it was coming. I would have said it myself had our positions been reversed.

"Chicken!"

For thousands of years, *chicken* has topped the list of the words most likely to provoke action from a nine-year-old boy. He might cry, he might bust you in the mouth, but if you call him a chicken, something will happen. That's certainly how I felt at that moment. Call me an ax murderer—call me a girl lover—but don't call me a chicken.

"Chicken!"

That did it. Furious, I turned around and made a wild dive for the rope.

Actually, the day had started off innocently enough. It was the Saturday before school was out for the summer. Jeff, Kevin, and I met on our bicycles in the woods behind Cabell's Gas Station.

"Well," Kevin said, "whatcha want to do?"

# Don't Call Me Chicken!

"Just hang out I guess," I replied. "Or we could build a fort."

"Forts are for babies," Jeff said frowning. "I ain't buildin' no fort."

"What about G. I. Joe?" I asked, "G. I. Joe builds forts, and he's not a baby." *Ah, that got him,* I thought. *It was so nice to be right.*

Jeff was a year older than Kevin and me, which, to his way of thinking, made him boss. We were somewhat skeptical of Jeff and his ideas because they always seemed to land us in trouble. The firecrackers in school? Jeff's idea. The rubber-band guns in church? Jeff's idea. The water balloon in the library, the dog on the basketball court, the tape recorder in my dad's bathroom? Jeff, Jeff, Jeff.

As I remember, it wasn't only the rope my father had warned me about. Jeff had been included as well. "He's not as smart as you think," Dad lectured. "If he was so sharp, he wouldn't have gotten caught with the money from the Coke machine."

I had to agree with that. For several months, Miss Luna Myers had reported money missing from the Coke machine at the county health department. Everybody in Sawyerton Springs knew it was happening. The story had even been reported in the *Sentinel.* "Who," the editorial page demanded, "was robbing the only Coke machine in town?"

Why, Jeff, of course. Or as the adults called him, "that Deas kid." He had been fishing change out of the machine with the blade from a hacksaw. He would've gotten away with it, too, if he hadn't wanted a pellet gun so badly. Jeff walked right into Tom Henley's Hardware Store, picked out the one he wanted, and paid Tom 49 dollars . . . in quarters!

Jeff was just that kind of kid. And that's what worried me as we sat there on our bikes. What would he come up with next? "We could have a dirt clod fight," he said, referring to an activity in which we collected lumps of earth from a freshly plowed field and threw them at each other.

"Nah," Kevin said, "I have on new pants. My mom'd kill me."

"Okay, then," Jeff countered, "how about we go to the Methodist Church and catch some goldfish?"

Kevin and I looked at each other and shrugged. "Awright," Kevin said. "Sure—let's go."

The Beauman's Pond United Methodist Church kept a goldfish pool in its prayer garden, which occasionally proved to be a temptation not easily overcome by boys my age.

Since my father was the minister at the Baptist church, I knew I would be in trouble if we were caught, but seeing as how they were Methodist fish . . . well, it wasn't actually a sin.

As we pedaled off, however, I couldn't help thinking of what my father always said about Jeff, which was "He's a good boy, but he needs some guidance." Then he'd say, "And if you hang around him too much, you're going to need some guidance, too." That worried me. Guidance from my dad often came in the form of a size 36, brown-and-black reversible belt.

I suppose I really should have stayed away from Jeff. Kevin's parents, too, had warned him about "wrong associations." It was just that Jeff had a special magnetism. Everything he came up with sounded exciting and wonderful. He could talk about snorkeling in a sewer, and by the time he was finished, you'd think it was a great idea!

We caught a couple of goldfish from the prayer garden pool, and, having the good sense not to take them home ("Hi Dad, I stole these! How about a whipping?"), we walked down to Beauman's Pond and released them.

We stood there wondering if the goldfish would be devoured by a giant bass or catfish. "Or maybe," Kevin mused, "one day somebody will catch a ten-pound goldfish in this very spot. Goldfish filets, mmm boy!" We all laughed.

Suddenly, Jeff looked across the pond and said, "Hey! Nobody's on the rope. Let's check it out."

As Jeff broke into a trot toward the General's Oak and Kevin immediately followed him, I began a conversation with myself. *Is this something you should be doing?* I asked. *Might this possibly lead to trouble? Could you fake a sprained ankle and bail out now?*

Quickly, I made my decision. "Hey guys," I yelled, "wait up!"

When I reached the tree, Jeff and Kevin were already under the rope, gazing up its incredible length. They were elbowing each other and chuckling. "Boy," Jeff said to me, "you sure were scared when you swung from the rope."

"I wasn't scared, " I said.

"Well, you sure were bawlin'," he said. He glanced toward Kevin, who was grinning weirdly.

"Who was bawlin'? I wasn't bawlin'," I said as I felt the heat rising on the back of my neck. I knew what he was doing, but I was powerless to stop it.

"Okay, if you weren't bawlin'," Jeff continued, "and you weren't scared . . . do it again."

"What?" I asked, trying to keep the fear from my voice.

"Do it again," Jeff demanded, "ride the rope!"

Thinking quickly, I said, "I can't. I haven't got my bathing suit."

With a gleam in his eye, Jeff went for his trump card. "You could take your clothes off—just go in your underwear. Nobody's around, but then . . . maybe you're chicken."

*What was I doing*, I wondered as I pulled off my clothes. I knew better than this. *Just stop!* I told myself. *Just stand up for once and say 'Jeff, I know what you're doing, and this time you won't get away with it.'* But I didn't, and he did. Moments later, I climbed the tree. And that's the story on how I got up there a second time.

"Chicken!"

Diving wildly for the rope was not one of my brighter moves that day. As I mentioned earlier, being identified as a member of the poultry family can severely affect the judgment of a boy. I was no exception. Leaping from the board platform was a mistake, and, having retained some degree of intelligence, it was a mistake I recognized immediately. I missed the rope by more than a foot.

Tumbling to the ground, bouncing from limb to limb, probably didn't take more than a few seconds, but believe me, it was enough time to reconsider the merits of rope swinging! Oddly enough, my overriding emotion was not one of fear, but of triumph. Oh, I was a goner, of that I was sure, but at least my tombstone would read HE WAS NOT A CHICKEN.

The point of this story is not that I might have been badly hurt (I wasn't) or whether or not my dad got after me with his belt (he did). The point, I suppose, is that as aggravating as certain kids are, they can still turn out all right.

Jeff Deas is now the police officer in Sawyerton Springs, and he's married with two children of his own. What most people saw in him as "trouble" was just creative energy.

Today, I am more likely to take an interest in a boy like Jeff. That mischievous attitude and all those wild ideas are leadership qualities in a child. Steered in the right direction, that kind of kid will eventually make our world a better place . . . if he doesn't drive us all crazy in the meantime!

"I'll let you use the car when you cut
your hair," Dad said.

# Dad Had the Keys to the Kingdom

"You remind me so much of your father." I hear that a lot from people who knew my dad. It is a compliment. Though appearance is a factor, I believe it to be the similarity in our personalities to which they are referring. My dad was a nut. Not a professional nut like I have become, but a nut none the less.

As I was growing up, he was the pastor, minister of music, and youth director at Grace Fellowship Baptist Church. My friends loved him. They had no choice—he made them laugh! Coming home from a date on any Friday night, I might find 20 kids at our house. They would all be gathered around my dad—all listening to him talk.

"I was a good student," he'd say. "I graduated from the seminary Magna Kum Bah Yah." Everyone would laugh, my mother would roll her eyes, and Dad would be on to something else!

"Speak French, Mr. Andrews," someone would say. He would do it.

"Russian!"

"Spanish!"

He "spoke" them, too. My father had never actually learned a foreign language, but he had a way of pronouncing individual syllables that seemed incredibly real. Using facial expressions and hand motions, he could convey his crazy thoughts—though no one ever understood a word! To my friends, it was the funniest thing in the world.

Miss Edna Thigpen of the *Sentinel* once asked to interview Dad during what he termed an unusually slow news week even for Sawyerton Springs. When word got out about the upcoming feature, the whole town was in a frenzy of anticipation. Everyone knew that "Brother Andrews" wasn't very tolerant of people who couldn't take a joke, and as he had stated on several occasions, "Miss Edna must've had her sense of humor removed as a child."

No one was disappointed with the article. It included Miss Edna's comments about how lucky the Baptists were to have a pastor who not only spoke 14 languages, including Swahili, but also to receive guidance from a man who often fished with Billy Graham! I have wondered many times if Dad ever asked forgiveness for those lies. I doubt it.

I was proud of the fact that even the "non-churchgoers" considered my father an okay guy. He was the best ping-pong player in town and was an above average second baseman on the Grace Fellowship softball team.

Dad didn't take hypocrisy lightly, and for a minister, he could be extremely direct. Early in his career, he spoke to a group of women who made up the Missionary Membership Committee, one of the most vocal (and volatile) forces a Baptist church ever generated. As local legend has it, he said, "Ladies, I have three things to tell you. Number one is that there are a lot of lost people in this world. Secondly, most of you don't give a damn about them. And thirdly," he added, noting the shock on their faces, "it is a shame that you care more about your pastor having said 'damn' than you do about all those lost people!"

I always chuckle when I think about that one.

My father also had different methods of parenting. While growing up, I received the usual number of spankings and lectures. The spankings ended when I was about 12, and although the lectures continued well into my teens, Dad often employed other disciplinary techniques.

One fall afternoon when I was in the eighth grade, Lee Peyton, Kevin Perkins, and I slipped down to the pond behind our house. Anxious to try out the corncob pipes we'd made the week before, we puffed the tobacco for about 20 minutes, threw up, and promised each other never to smoke again. After tossing all the evidence into the water, we ate a package of breath mints and forgot the whole episode.

Several days later, Lee and Kevin were at my house watching television. Dad came into the room and sat down for a few minutes. Then, as he left, he tossed us a small photo album and said, "Hey, take a look at the new pictures I just had developed."

We shrugged our shoulders and began thumbing through them. It was the usual family stuff. Our dog, my mother and her azalea bush, my sister's birthday party, some kids smoking beside a pond. What! We looked closer. Oh my gosh! That was us! But how?

Suddenly, it was clear. My father had crept through the woods, eased down to the pond, and from behind a tree, taken a perfectly focused (suitable for framing) picture of us and the cloud of smoke around our heads. He never said another word about the incident, but the message was clear: I wasn't getting away with anything!

And believe me, I rarely tried. Dad wasn't all fun and games. He had certain rules that were unbreakable. "Unbreakable," he would say, "unless you want to be broken!" He was only kidding. (I think.)

Number One: "You will stand when a lady walks into the room. This includes your sister and your mother."

Dad was sure that my wife would appreciate him for that rule one day. He was right.

Number Two: "You will eat some of everything that is being served. You will eat everything on your plate."

Dad, having been born during the Depression, was big on this one, but I was such a picky eater that this rule was no longer in effect by the time my sister arrived. I think "the big liver stand-off of 1965" must have worn him down.

Number Three: "Do not hit your sister."

This was (no contest) the hardest rule to obey. My sister never had a "do not hit your brother" rule, and subsequently she did so quite often. This, by the way, is the only rule in which I still do not see the wisdom!

Number Four: "Never play in the living room with firecrackers, water balloons, mud, skates, a yoyo, a bullwhip, or the dog."

This rule actually started out as plain old "never play in the living room." All the other things were added one at a time!

Number Five: "Always tell the truth. Half the truth is a lie."

I'm not sure if he would appreciate how closely I am adhering to this rule while writing a story about him! Sorry, Dad.

On most Sunday mornings, my father walked to church. He said it was to clear his mind and make final edits in his sermon. By 11:00, every pew would be packed with people waiting to hear "what Brother Andrews has come up with this week." For the most part, the congregation enjoyed his messages, but he had his detractors, too.

Some thought Dad was irreverent—that he was not respectful enough. Once, a visiting preacher concluded his sermon by yelling to everyone that all the televisions should be thrown into the river, all the stereos and radios should be thrown into the

# Dad Had the Keys to the Kingdom

river, and that all the miniskirts and bikinis should be thrown into the river. When finally he sat down, Dad approached the pulpit and said, "Please rise and join me now in singing hymn number 481: "Shall We Gather at the River."

He once urged his flock not to tell the Methodists that to get into heaven they would need to be carrying a covered dish! These were the kinds of things that made people love my dad. He was convinced that God knew how to smile.

I'll never forget a conversation with my father that occurred shortly after I had gotten my driver's license. I had asked him for the keys to the car when he offered, "I'll let you use the car when you cut your hair."

Thinking I had him cornered, I said, "But, Dad, Jesus had long hair."

"Yes," my father agreed, "he did." Then, with a smile he added, "He also walked everywhere he went!"

My father certainly knew how to laugh, and his smile was his greatest asset. I can only hope to be the kind of man he was: generous, witty, kind, and consistent. He was a great dad, and I wish he were still around. I miss him a bunch during holidays, Father's Day being especially tough.

I suppose I miss him most when I am reminded of his sense of humor. That is, after all, his legacy to me. "Laughter," he would say, "is also a ministry."

*Clenching his teeth, Bubba demanded,*
*"Are you saying that I'm not intelligent?"*

# The Grave Decision

A fist fight almost broke out in Sawyerton Springs a few days ago. Billy Pat Williams and Bubba Pratt, despite being neighbors and long-time friends, very nearly got into it. They were right on Main Street, across from Henley's Hardware, when it started.

"Well," Billy Pat said, "Me'n Ginny are going to vote 'yes' and just hope there are enough other intelligent people in town to push this thing through."

Clenching his teeth, Bubba demanded, "Are you saying that I'm not intelligent?"

"Draw your own conclusions," Billy Pat retorted.

The next thing anyone knew, they were shoving like school kids and saying things like "Oh, yeah?" and "I dare ya." Thankfully, cooler heads prevailed and the two were pulled apart before anyone got punched, but no one bothered to ask what in the heck was going on—everyone knew.

The whole thing started last Monday night when Roger Luker showed up at a town council meeting. Roger arrived late and sat near the back of the room.

Meetings of the town council have been little more than a social event for years. Time and again, people come to hash over the same old things—parking problems, littering fines, and property tax disputes. They all seem to enjoy it—just bicker a while, drink some coffee, and go home.

Roger waited anxiously for Rick Carper to quit arguing about the lack of a leash law in the city limits and smiled at Miss Luna Myers across the aisle. She and Miss Edna Thigpen were there to air their monthly gripe about the inconsistencies of garbage pick-up. *Just about everybody in town is here tonight*, Roger thought to himself as he glanced around the room.

As he stood up to speak, his knees felt weak. Roger's wife, Carol, hadn't accompanied him to the meeting because she didn't approve of what he was about to announce. Putting her out of his mind, he cleared his throat and said, "Members of the council, I'm Roger Luker of Roger Luker Real Estate. . . ."

"Excuse me," Dick Rollins interrupted, "What company did you say you were with?" Everyone in the room laughed as Roger's face reddened. They all knew very well who he was and what he did. After all, Roger had grown up here. It just tickled them that someone they had known for 37 years would feel compelled to announce his name and business every time he shook your hand!

As the room settled down, Roger ignored the snickers and continued. "I have," he said, "from an outside business interest, a proposal to build a golf course around Beauman's Pond and develop the Springs as a resort."

As if someone had flipped a switch, the room was instantly silent. Several men, frowning, rose slightly in their seats. Even the ladies working at the coffee table froze in mid-pour. You could literally hear everyone swallowing . . . hard.

If it was their attention Roger was after, he got it. He might as well have said, "I'm Roger Luker of Roger Luker Real Estate, and I'm here to take your children!" The reaction would not have been any different.

From that point on, the meeting was an exercise in finger pointing and name calling until they all got tired and went home. Roger, having seen the handwriting on the wall, left within minutes of his announcement.

He gunned his Ford Galaxy up the big hill on Cherokee Avenue and squealed the tires as he turned onto Keating. Passing Dick Rollins' house, he muttered under his breath, "Jerk," and then, reaching the last house on the right, skidded into his own driveway.

Roger slammed the screen door as he stalked inside, and to Carol, who was sitting on the couch with her arms folded, he said, "Buncha hicks!" Carol simply looked at him. Her lips were pursed and her gaze steady. She made no comment. "They're all a buncha hicks," he said a little louder this time. Carol still didn't say anything, so Roger went to bed.

Roger and Carol have lived in the same three-bedroom, two-bath house since they got married 12 years ago. They have two children—Ben, a three-year-old boy, and Kelsey, a baby girl. They have a good marriage, but their personalities couldn't be more different.

Carol is satisfied with her home, her town, her family, and life in general. Roger, on the other hand, is professionally bored. Since 1976, he has been the only real estate agent in a town that never saw a house bigger than three bedrooms. For years, he has dreamed of the big deal, until out of the blue, Thursday of a week ago, the deal walked through the door.

A distinguished looking man wearing an expensive suit and alligator shoes showed up without an appointment and asked to see the springs for which the town was named. Did the springs flow from marsh or rock? Was the water pure? Who owned the springs? Who owned the land nearby? Explaining that he represented a large development firm in Atlanta, he described to Roger the type of area for which he was searching.

Roger immediately drove him to the springs. Located behind the Beauman's Pond United Methodist Church, the springs fed Beauman's Pond and provided water for the whole town. The springs, the pond, and 129 surrounding acres were deeded to the town by Thornton Beauman more than one hundred years ago. Technically, the town also owned the land on which the Methodist Church stood, but that had never been a problem.

After walking the property, taking some pictures, and talking into a little tape recorder every few steps, the man asked to be driven back to his car, which was still at Roger's office. As he made ready to leave, he turned to Roger and said, "We are prepared to offer a five percent ownership package and $700,000 to the town of Sawyerton Springs for the total parcel of land. The payment would be a one-time cash deal with the ownership package including residual revenues from a resort hotel and golf course. I'll need a commitment, in writing, two weeks from today."

And with that, the man drove away. Roger ran inside, locked the door, and quickly began calculating what his commission would be on $700,000. "Two weeks," he said to himself. "I have two weeks to get this done."

By 9:00 on the morning after the council meeting, every man, woman, and child in town had an opinion about Roger Luker. To some, he was an economic savior, to others, he was Benedict Arnold in a leisure suit!

Billy Pat Williams and his wife, Ginny, were among those who liked the idea of development. "It'd be good for business in this area," Billy Pat said, "and besides, I always wanted to play golf."

Tom Henley was also for the deal. He carried golf balls in his hardware store, and in 17 years had not sold the first one.

Bubba Pratt and Dick Rollins led the group of business owners who wanted to call the man from Atlanta, tell him no, thank you, and then "just go beat the crud out of Roger."

Also committed to preserving the status quo were the ladies of the Genealogical Society led by Miss Luna Myers and Miss Edna

Thigpen. They made signs and formed a picket line around Beauman's Pond. The signs were printed with slogans like "S. O. S . . . Save Our Springs" and "Golfers Gamble and Curse—Do We Want That Here?"

Miss Edna, as editor of the *Sawyerton Springs Sentinel*, dedicated an entire edition to the controversy. Included were pictures of families picnicking at the pond and by the springs and comments by some of the townsfolk who were against the change. Dr. Lee Peyton said that if he'd wanted to live in a town with strangers, he would have moved to Birmingham in the first place.

Conspicuously absent in the paper was any opposing viewpoint. "I own the darn thing," Miss Edna said, "I'll put in it what I want!" And she did. The prize piece of writing, however, belonged to Miss Luna. In her weekly column "What's On My Mind," she really let everyone know. It was a scathing diatribe on developers, Roger Luker, and change in general. She even mentioned Satan several times. Near the end of her column, Miss Luna asked the question, "When the whole place is destroyed with swimming pools, tennis courts, and golf courses—what will be left for our children to do?"

Actually, Miss Luna made an observation that had been overlooked. What about the church? The Beauman's Pond United Methodist Church had stood in the same location since the 1920s. Was it now in danger of being used as a clubhouse? "Or," Miss Luna wondered, "will the sinners just tear it down? . . . And what about the cemetery behind the church? Will they allow us to dig up our loved ones, or will they use the headstones as hazards on the golf course like a sand trap or a lake?"

Yesterday, when the town council announced that the residents of Sawyerton Springs had voted unanimously to reject the offer of development, most people admitted that what was on Miss Luna's mind had kind of been on theirs, too. Everyone had been waiting outside the meeting hall for the results, and even Billy Pat and Tom expressed relief that they weren't the only ones to have changed their minds.

As the crowd was breaking up, Billy Pat yelled, "Hey everybody, hang on a second!" As they all froze, Billy Pat turned to find Roger, who had been standing off to the side. Looking right at him, Billy Pat said, "The council just told us that the vote was unanimous." Billy Pat paused as his eyes narrowed. "Which means that you must've. . . ." Suddenly, he grinned. "Well, at least tell us why you voted against yourself."

"I'm not sure," Roger said smiling sheepishly. "I suppose it had something to do with my growing up here. I got to thinking about playing golf and tennis with my kids, and I realized that there are a million places to do those things. But you know, there's only one place I can show them where I used to swing on a rope with my friends. There's only one place I caught salamanders with my dad. There's only one church I've ever been a member of. And," he said softly as he took Carol's hand, "there's only one place that I can show them where their parents got engaged. Sawyerton Springs is my hometown."

Well, of course, Roger is back in everyone's good graces. And he's no longer professionally bored. The town doesn't know it yet, but Roger has decided to build a course anyway. He has already made an offer on the land next to his office, and the first tee will start within sight of his front door. It will be perfect for families— 18 beautifully landscaped holes . . . of miniature golf.

*They entered the den screaming at the top of their lungs. "Kill it, Billy Pat! Help! Oh, Lord! Help! Kill it!"*

# Shootout in Sawyerton Springs

I have spoken with several residents of Sawyerton Springs this week, and without exception, they all agreed that the Big Annual Chamber of Commerce Dance last Saturday night had been a huge success. Rebecca Peyton and Glenda Perkins headed up the women's committee, which raised enough money to bring in a professional band all the way from North Carolina.

The group, Carl Benson's Wildcats, usually plays high school reunions in the Raleigh area, but Rebecca, having seen them on a local television show, was determined to book them for this year's event. At first, everyone had been disappointed because Carl was sick and didn't make the trip. Carl's mother, however, was a "more than ample" substitute on the saxophone.

Everyone in town was there. After all, the Big Annual Chamber of Commerce Dance is the social event of the year. This is the chance to see and be seen. It is also the starting point for a world of gossip: "Isn't that the same powder-blue tux that Dick Rollins wore in his son's wedding last year? Seems kind of a sleazy color. I thought so then, and I think so now. He looks like the doorman in a strip joint."

"What's with Sandy Pratt and that new necklace? Bubba took her to Orlando in July, and they're going to New Orleans before Thanksgiving. I don't care what anybody says, they're getting money from somewhere besides that chicken stand!"

Even Lee Peyton was not immune to the rumor mill. Being a doctor, he is watched closely, and though he only had one glass of wine all night, by noon the next day, everyone had heard that he'd been "drunker'n Cooter Brown."

Tom and Terri Henley, Rick and Sue Carper, Roger and Carol Luker were all there and had a wonderful time. The only damper on the evening came during the hour that Miss Edna Thigpen and Miss Luna Myers made their appearances. Because every breath a person takes ends up in the *Sentinel*, people were simply too nervous to have fun.

Billy Pat and Ginny Williams arrived late and left early. Billy Pat has been putting in a lot of hours down at the dealership, and he came home Saturday with a migraine. Ginny had her heart set on the dance, though, so he went and gamely stayed as long as he could. It was about the fourth time Carl Benson's mother did an encore on the same song that Billy Pat decided he'd had all he could take. "Hunk-a hunk-a burnin' love," he said, "just don't get it on the saxophone!"

On the way home, they didn't really talk much. Ginny wasn't mad—it was just that she'd looked forward to spending the evening out. In Sawyerton Springs, it isn't every night—or even every Saturday night—when there is something to do.

As they pulled into their driveway, she noted that Miss Edna and Miss Luna, in the house across the street, were already home.

# Shootout in Sawyerton Springs

Having the two older ladies so close, Ginny figured, could be considered both good and bad. And actually, the good part and the bad part were one and the same!

That, of course, has to do with the fact that Miss Edna and Miss Luna never miss anything. Ever. On the one hand, that is a plus. Keating Drive doesn't need a watchdog. But on the other hand, it can be a nuisance. If something (anything) doesn't seem right to them, they never hesitate to call.

The phone will ring.

"Ginny?"

"Yes, Miss Edna," Ginny will sigh.

"Ginny, it's certainly none of my concern, but there is a boy outside cutting your bushes, and I thought you should be aware of it."

"Yes, ma'am," Ginny will respond, "we know. Billy Pat's paying him to do it."

Or one of them might catch Billy Pat at church.

"Billy Pat?"

"Yes, Miss Luna?"

"I couldn't help but notice the amount of your tithe check as the offering plate passed me today. I'm overjoyed your business is doing so well!"

In any case, both of them are 83 years old. And as Billy Pat and Ginny keep reminding themselves, "It's just a blessing they're still with us."

Heading in through the front door, Billy Pat almost tripped over the broom he'd left on the porch earlier that day. He cussed, kicked it, and left it there. Once inside, he got out of his suit, fed their dog Barney, and after taking two Sominex tablets and several aspirin, crawled into bed.

Ginny, trying her best to keep out of his way, stayed up and watched the late show—G-Men, starring James Cagney. It was well after midnight when she put on her long, flannel nightgown and eased under the covers beside Billy Pat. He was sleeping soundly, she noted with some relief, and within minutes, Ginny was asleep as well.

Until 2:13 a.m., the only sound in the Williams' house was Billy Pat's quiet snoring and the occasional squeaking noise as Barney shifted positions on the foot of the bed. At 2:14, however, shattering the silence like a bullwhip, the phone rang.

Instinctively, Ginny made a grab at the sound and turned over the glass of water on her night table. "Hello," she answered groggily as she finally found the receiver. "Yes, Miss Luna." Billy Pat groaned. Suddenly, Ginny kicked the covers off and turned on the lamp. "Stay in your room, Miss Luna. We'll be right over!"

"Get up, Billy Pat," Ginny said loudly as she punched him in the back. "Miss Luna says something's in their house!"

Billy Pat was still half asleep, and the combination of Sominex and his wife's fist had him thoroughly confused. "What's in their house?" he asked.

"Something! Just something, Billy Pat. Get up, NOW!" Ginny was already at the bedroom door.

As Billy Pat rolled out of bed and fumbled for his pants, Ginny yelled, "NO TIME!" and pushed her bathrobe into his arms. It was bright pink with yellow flowers, and as he struggled to put it on, she herded him out the front door.

Reaching the yard, Billy Pat stopped. "Now hold on, daggummit," he said. "Just what the heck are we walking into here? Exactly what is 'something'? Are we talking about an escapee from the crazy house, an ax murderer, or just your ordinary gang of killers?"

"Go," Ginny said, "and be careful. I'll call the police." And with that, she pulled the broom off the porch and put it in his hands.

"Oh, great," Billy Pat muttered to himself as he crossed the street, "this'll be a big help."

There was one more thing on Billy Pat's mind at that moment. He had taken a lot of teasing last year when he was seen breaking up a dogfight in the middle of the night. At the time, he was wearing his boxer shorts and wielding an American flag. Ginny's bathrobe and this broom, he knew, would not help his image.

Entering through the side door with the key under the mat, Billy Pat went directly to the bedroom. Miss Edna and Miss Luna, their hair done up in curlers, were cowering in fright between the twin beds. Over and over they pointed down the hall and stammered, "The den. Something's in the den."

The door to the den was slightly ajar. Peering into the spacious room, Billy Pat noticed the lamp that had been left on in the corner. Its glow allowed him to see almost everything. In fact, the only area he could not see was behind the big sofa that faced him. That, Billy Pat reasoned, was the only place someone might be hiding.

Billy Pat cleared his throat. He stamped his foot. Nothing. "All right," he said in a loud voice, "I've got you covered. Come on out." He desperately hoped no one would. They didn't.

Over his shoulder he shouted, "Johnny! Frank! We're not getting any cooperation—looks like we'll have to bring in the Dobermans!" He waited.

Relatively convinced that no one was behind the sofa, Billy Pat eased into the den. Suddenly, without warning, from the right side of the room, the "something" appeared in Billy Pat's face. Instinctively, he ducked and swung the broom, knocking Miss Luna's bowling trophys off the television set.

"It's a flying squirrel," he howled as he swung again. "It's a dang flying squirrel!" Now Billy Pat was mad. All the stress of the past few minutes—feeling as though he might be gunned down any second, not to mention the lack of sleep—he was going to take it out on the squirrel.

As Billy Pat chased the animal around the den, he continued to shout, "It's a flying squirrel," trying to let Miss Edna and Miss Luna know that they had nothing to fear. It didn't work. Evidently, both ladies have an acute phobia that is directly related to rodents, and, unfortunately, as far as they were concerned, this was just a rat with wings.

They entered the den screaming at the top of their lungs, "Kill it, Billy Pat! Help! Oh, Lord! Help! Kill it!"

Billy Pat was trying. He broke the light fixture on the ceiling with a backswing, and as the terrified creature scampered across the coffee table, he cleared that piece of furniture with one mighty blow. He missed the squirrel, but an old candy jar, several pictures of relatives, and a miniature gong all ended up on the floor.

At some point during all this ruckus, Miss Luna gave Billy Pat the old .22 rifle she keeps in her closet. "It is already loaded," she said. "Use it and save us all!"

Though Billy Pat had the gun in his hands, it wasn't his intention to actually fire it. When the squirrel came at them again, however, and the hysterical ladies yelled "SHOOT," he did!

POW! He hit the lamp in the corner. "Shoot, Billy Pat, shoot!" POW! POW! Feathers flew everywhere as two sofa pillows bit the dust. "Help! Kill it, Billy Pat! Help! Shoot! Shoot!" POW, POW, POW, POW, POW!

What with the panic stricken women and the sound of his own shots, Billy Pat had lost all control. When the squirrel ran along a curtain rod, he splintered the pine board paneling above it and put three holes in the window, but the rifle, at last, was empty.

Well, it worked. Before the police arrived, the flying squirrel had sailed into the night. He was not harmed and probably told his family a better story than the one Sawyerton Springs is talking about!

And are they ever talking about it! When the *Sentinel* came out yesterday, Billy Pat was fairly certain the town would forget the dogfight. There, on the front page, was the story of THE SHOOTOUT ON KEATING DRIVE, complete with an artist's rendering of Billy Pat in the bathrobe—rifle in one hand, broom in the other. The caption read: "Go Ahead, Squirrel. Make My Day."

As Steve continued to mouth nonexistent
words, I quickly turned around and
almost fainted. There, sliding slowly
through the window, was a pitchfork.

# Crazy Hazey Forks Over the Head

"Who stole my golden arm?" At that moment, I was not happy with the decision I'd made that afternoon to spend the night in the old Hazey place.

"Who stole my golden arm?"

Kevin Perkins held a flashlight to his face and was making an effort to scare me. It was working.

Suddenly, he shut off the light, grabbed at me, and screamed, "You stole my golden arm!"

In a split second, my hands were over my face. My leg kicked into the air as I lurched against the wall and yelled, "Ahh!" Then, slowly, I gathered my composure and explained my actions, which had, obviously, been for the benefit of the story—the better to scare everyone else.

It was a lame excuse, and Lee Peyton said so. The Luker boys, Steve and Roger, agreed as Kevin looked at me smugly. "You were spooked," he said, "You're always spooked when we come here."

He was right. I had been in the house a hundred times, but it still gave me the willies. Located at the end of a logging road behind town, the dilapidated old structure had been abandoned for years. It was covered with wandering fingers of kudzu and honeysuckle, which only added to its creepy appearance.

The house held a sinister attraction for kids. Despite the pitch-fork murder that had supposedly taken place in the attic at one time, we simply could not stay away.

This night, however, was different. I could have easily stayed away. In fact, on this particular night, I would have rather been anywhere else in the world. Because this night was the 31st of October—Halloween.

For the first time any of us could remember, Halloween was happening on a Friday. That meant, of course, no school the next day. We were given permission by our parents to camp out in the Peyton's backyard, and the tent, in fact, was there. We, on the other hand, were not.

Somehow, the five of us had goaded each other into spending the night at the old Hazey place. We considered ourselves too mature for dressing up and begging candy from the neighbors.

Not that we didn't get candy anyway. Every Halloween, it amazed us that there were adults so naive as to leave a bowl of candy on the porch with a note saying "Take One, Please." Two or three spots like that and a kid was done for the night!

We sat in a tight circle, close together in what we had decided was once the living area. There was a crumbling fireplace at one end of the room with an ancient sofa nearby. Directly behind us was the small staircase that led to the attic. "Dad will have a spaz attack if he finds out about this," Roger said. We all looked at him.

Steve, his older brother, spoke first. "You know what I'm gonna do if he finds out?"

"Kill me?" Roger asked.

# Crazy Hazey Forks Over the Head

"Right," Steve confirmed.

We were quiet for a while. I, for one, was not enjoying myself and would have gladly paid Roger to go get his dad. The stories were beginning to have an effect on me. I had had enough golden arms, hooks left hanging on car doors, and ghost girls being picked up on the highway wearing prom dresses. I was ready to leave and was about to suggest it when Lee picked up the conversation. "Reckon why she did it?" he asked.

We all looked at him. We knew what he was talking about. In 1951, so the story went, Martha Hazey stuck her fourth husband, George, with a pitchfork in the attic.

"She must have been really upset," Lee said.

"Not as upset as George, I'll bet," Kevin said, laughing nervously.

"Her first three husbands died from eating poisoned mushrooms," I said, repeating what I'd heard from Wayne Gardner at school.

"Well then, why'd she kill poor George?" Roger asked.

Steve smirked, "Prob'ly 'cause he wouldn't eat the mushrooms!"

"My Dad said she cut off his head," Lee offered. In our hearts, we knew that Lee's father had said nothing of the kind—that Lee had fabricated this part of the story, but no one challenged him, because the information, according to Lee, had come from his dad. Crediting one's parent with a wild tale has always been the number-one method for avoiding the scorn of peers. ("I didn't say it, my dad said it!")

"Martha Hazey," I mused. "What kind of name is Hazey?"

"I'll betcha God gave her that name," Kevin said, "because it rhymes with crazy. You know she escaped from an insane asylum."

Kevin made the statement as a fact. He was not asking us if Crazy Hazey had escaped—he was telling us that indeed, she had. He continued. "She dug up George's head and still carries it around . . . everywhere she goes." I was about to tell Kevin that he was full of it when he added, "At least, that's what my mother told me."

"Somebody saw her down at Henley's Hardware not too long ago," I said. "She was looking around in the pitchfork section."

The other guys looked at me. Their eyes were the size of silver dollars and their breath was coming in rapid bursts. They knew I was lying as well as I did, but as we embellished the tale, it was like an addiction—there was no stopping us. The tension became unbearable. Past the point of casually getting up and going home, we were terrified!

Suddenly, Roger began to sing. "A hundred bottles of beer on the wall, a hundred bottles of beer. Take one down, pass it around. . . ." As his quivering voice faded away, we felt even more uneasy. It had been a pitiful attempt to change the subject. Roger was embarrassed, and we were embarrassed for him.

Only Roger's brother, Steve, said anything to him. "Don't be so stupid. If you ever do anything that stupid again, I'll. . . ." Without warning, Steve's face went white. His mouth kept moving, but there were no words—no sound. He was looking at a spot directly behind me.

I looked at Roger and Lee. Their eyes were now fixed on the same spot. Roger was on his back trying to push himself away with his legs. Lee didn't move.

Kevin started a weird moaning sound that seemed a combination of crying and begging for mercy. As Steve continued to mouth nonexistent words, I quickly turned around and almost fainted. There, sliding slowly through the window, was a pitchfork.

My mouth was like sand and my heart was about to come through my chest. It was true! All the stories we'd heard were true. There really was a Crazy Hazey. She really did kill her husband, and now she was after us! Why had I come here? Why hadn't I gone trick or treating with my sister? Oh, if only I was wearing my Lone Ranger costume, but it was too late—we were goners!

"Ahh!" Kevin screamed, "It's George's head!" Indeed, something that looked very much like a man's head had come flying through the window and rolled up against Lee's leg.

A large percentage of the time, when one speaks of "hair standing on end," it is merely a figure of speech. In this case, it was not. Our hair did stand on end, we curdled blood with our screams, and before we left the house, we ran in place for a few seconds like mice in a cartoon!

We didn't stop running until we were safely in the Peyton's backyard. We were out of breath, we were still scared, but we were alive.

To this day, I have never experienced sheer terror to match that Halloween. Even now, I get shivers when I hear "Hundred Bottles of Beer on the Wall." That song will forever be known to me as the "Pitchfork Prelude."

It wasn't until years later—I was in college, actually—when I found out what had happened that night. My mom and dad had walked over to the Peyton's with my sister, who was dressed as a dog. As the adults talked in the side yard, they saw us leaving the tent. Dr. Peyton and my dad decided to follow.

They had waited outside the window of the old Hazey place listening to us talk in the living room. When the time was right, Dr. Peyton stuck an old board slowly into the window. (This is where I differ with my father's version. I still swear it was a pitchfork. "Where would we get a pitchfork in the middle of the night?" my father said.) Then my dad threw a clump of roots into the room, and the rest is history.

Because of that night, I never went in the old Hazey place again. That, I am sure, is exactly what my dad had intended. If so, he accomplished his goal. Still, it was a mean trick for a grownup to play on a bunch of kids. It makes no difference that it was Halloween. It was dirty, rotten, heartless . . . and I can't wait for the chance to do something like that to a boy of my own!

As he sat there, hunkered down in some
blackberry briars, it began to rain. It
was just a drizzle, but soon Jerry was
miserably soaked.

# Ducking the Game Warden

The temperature was hovering around 27 degrees, which is cold for the Springs area, but not cold enough to keep Kevin Perkins indoors. For most of his life, he has hunted mallards, pintails, and woodies on the backwaters of Beauman's Pond, and, as far as he was concerned, this was the most important time of the year. It was the week before Christmas—the last gasp of duck season.

Kevin was on his way to The Last Resort, a cabin deep in the woods that his father had built when Kevin was a boy. As he nudged his Jeep across a pine tree that had fallen in the dirt road, Kevin smiled. He would soon be meeting the whole gang. Every year, they spent this week together in the woods. And, seeing as how this was the week before Christmas, their wives always had a collective fit.

Glenda had really given it to him before they left. It was the same things she said every year. "I can't believe you're leaving. Here it is the busiest week of the year. Do you realize how much has to be done before everyone shows up on Christmas Eve? Do you not have any consideration for me at all?"

Kevin frowned. He did hate to leave Glenda—at this time of the year especially—but he simply had no choice. He was only doing what his father had done year after year. It was a tradition, and he was not about to break it.

Rounding the last curve in the muddy road, Kevin saw smoke coming from the chimney, then the cabin itself. It was only three rooms, and what with the green paint flaking, it looked abandoned. But to Kevin, Bubba Pratt, Jeff Deas, Billy Pat Williams, and Dick Rollins it was a paradise.

The guys piled out the front (and only) door as Kevin parked. "How boutcha, old man," Bubba said as he grabbed Kevin's duffel from the back seat. Kevin was "old man" to his friends. Not because of his age—he wasn't that old. It was what they had been calling him since the tenth grade when he began losing his hair.

Dick and Jeff ran around to the other side of the Jeep. "We'll get your gun," Jeff said.

"You guys leave my gun alone," Kevin shouted as he reached in and pulled the 12-gauge through his door. Several years before, on opening day, Dick and Jeff had removed the firing pins from Kevin's shotguns. The guns would not shoot, so Kevin was the designated caller for his buddies all day long. Kevin was a good sport about it, but he had not forgotten.

"Where's Billy Pat?" Kevin asked.

"Oh, he's a weenie," Jeff said, laughing. "Ginny told him he wasn't going anywhere. She said that the garage had needed cleaning since August and that she'd be danged if he was comin' with us."

"I blew the horn at him when I drove by," Dick said. "He had a

# Ducking the Game Warden

lamp under his arm." They all chuckled.

"He'll wish he'd of stood up to her in the morning," Bubba said. "We're gonna get a thousand ducks!"

"You better be careful," Kevin said as he smiled and looked toward the woods. "You wouldn't want Jerry to hear you say that."

They all nodded. They certainly didn't want Jerry to hear anything about a thousand ducks, a hundred ducks, or even one measly duck over the limit. Jerry was the game warden.

Jerry Anderson and his wife, Katrina, live on Randal Road right behind Dick and his family. They go to Grace Fellowship Baptist Church where Jerry teaches Sunday School and Katrina sings in the choir. Jerry is active in civic affairs, and he is Jeff Deas' best friend—11 months out of the year.

During hunting season, Jerry has a reputation as a tough customer. "You wouldn't even know he's my friend at all," Jeff told the guys. "The man takes his job seriously. He'd give me a ticket in a heartbeat."

"I am a conservation officer," Jerry would say. "I am paid to protect the laws of our state as they apply to game and fish. And I'm gonna do it. If my own mother shot a duck out of season, I'd write her a ticket." The whole town agreed that, yes, he would.

Jerry is a full-blooded Choctaw Indian and he knows that gives him an advantage in the woods. Not that he is quieter or has a better sense of direction than the next guy—it's just that he is the only Native American that most people in Sawyerton Springs have ever met, so everyone thinks that his skills are on a different level.

And he doesn't do anything to discourage their thinking. Occasionally, when he is in the woods with a friend, Jerry will feel the ground and say something like, "Deer. Two. Came through about an hour ago. The big one has a nice rack." Then he'll just walk on as if he could tell you what they ate for breakfast.

Because of Jerry's devotion to his career, people are a little nervous around him during hunting season. It's not that they're intending to break the law, it's just that he watches so closely.

Inside the cabin, over supper that night, Jerry was still the topic of conversation. "I knew a guy one time," Bubba said, "that swore Jerry came up out of the ground to get him. Swore he just appeared."

"It's the Indian in him," Dick said. "Tonto was like that."

Kevin looked puzzled. "Who?" he asked.

"Tonto," Dick said. "You know, Tonto, the Lone Ranger's friend."

Jeff spoke up: "You know the Lone Ranger killed Tonto."

"I didn't know that," Bubba said. "Why'd he do it?"

Jeff smirked. "He finally found out what *Kemosabe* meant!"

Just then, Billy Pat walked through the door. "Well, well," Kevin said. "We didn't think we were gonna see you this week."

"You had nothing to worry about," Billy Pat said as he sat down at the table. "I told Ginny that I was coming and that was that. 'Ginny,' I said, 'I'm running the show around here, and if I want to go hunting with the guys, then I'm going hunting with the guys, and there's nothing you or anybody else can do about it. Goodbye, baby,' I said, and here I am."

Kevin, Bubba, Dick, and Jeff looked at Billy Pat for a long moment. Kevin spoke. "You finished the garage, right?"

Billy Pat nodded. "And the basement," he said.

The week went by fast, and the hunting was terrific. They never saw Jerry, but they were fairly certain that he was around. One reason they had gotten nervous about Jerry's presence over the years was the law about legal shooting light.

Legal shooting time actually began well after daybreak; a law most hunters in the area had decided was unfair. The ducks had already landed by the time anyone could legally shoot. Therefore, a man who wouldn't dream of shooting over the limit would often, without guilt, start shooting as soon as he could see.

This was accepted behavior for the inhabitants of The Last Resort. They felt that an unfair law didn't really apply in their situation. Jerry, on the other hand, felt that it did.

# Ducking the Game Warden

"I'm going to get those jokers," Jerry told Katrina as they went to bed that night. "I hear them shooting too early every day, but by the time I can locate and sneak up on them, it's legal to shoot. I've got to actually catch them in the act."

At 2 a.m., Jerry sat up in bed. "I've got it. I'll beat 'em to the punch. See you later, honey," he said as he crawled out of bed.

Jerry planned to hide outside the cabin, waiting for the guys to wake up. Then, as they left to hunt, he would simply follow them to their duck blind and ticket them when they started shooting.

Slipping into position about 50 feet from the cabin door, Jerry shivered. It was almost 3 o'clock and pitch-black dark. He had a while to wait before they woke up.

As he sat there, hunkered down in some blackberry briars, it began to rain. It was just a drizzle, but soon Jerry was miserably soaked. His only consolation was the glory of his mission. He tried to imagine what it would be like when he revealed himself to the lawbreakers.

*Smile, I'll say*, Jerry thought, *you're on "Candid Camera." No, That's too much of a cliché. That show has been off the air for 20 years. I could sneak up right behind them and blow on a duck call as loud as I can. But no,* he decided, *they'd probably turn around and shoot me.*

After exploring options for about an hour, Jerry determined that the best method of surprising the guys would be to crawl beside the blind and just stand up. Jerry chuckled to himself. Whenever he did that, people looked at him as if he had come out of the ground.

At exactly 3:50 a.m., lights came on in the cabin, and Jerry was alert. He could hear Kevin singing "Onward Christian Soldiers" at the top of his lungs. Pots and pans began to rattle as Bubba started the bacon and grits. Jeff stood on the front porch and smoked a cigarette.

Turning to go inside, Jeff flicked the cigarette butt in Jerry's direction. *I ought to stand up now*, Jerry thought. *I could get him for littering.*

At that very moment, Kevin came to the door. He leaned outside and yelled, "Hey, Jerry! Man, don't sit out there in the rain. Come on in and have some breakfast!"

Jerry's mouth dropped open. "Unbelievable," he mumbled as he stiffly rose out of the briars. Walking toward the cabin, he was almost in shock. Kevin shoved a chair toward him as he went inside. Bubba handed him a plate.

Dick and Billy Pat sat on the other side of the table from Jerry. Neither could stop grinning. Jeff slapped Jerry on the back and laughed out loud.

"How?" Jerry asked. "How could you have possibly known I was out there?"

"Should we tell him?" Kevin directed his question to the other men in the room. They nodded.

"Jerry," Kevin said, smiling, "we actually had no idea you were waiting for us. But in a way, I guess you could say we've been waiting for you. We've been calling you to breakfast for the past 13 years!"

*Sharon Holbert was howling, Jeff Deas
was beating his desk, and Miss Wheeler
was standing in the middle of it all with
an open English book, looking at me.*

# Wonderful Wheeler and the Flat-Out Lie

Never in my life had I encountered such beauty. Her perfect face, framed by long, blond hair, featured the most incredible green eyes I had ever seen. Her voice was a symphony and her movements . . . hypnotic.

"Linda Gail," I wanted to say, "I love you. You were meant to be mine." And then I would kiss her. And not just anywhere either. I would kiss her—on the mouth!

Faintly, I thought, I could hear giggling. "Andy? Andy!" Looking up, I saw that wonderful face. She looked worried.

I said, "What's wrong, Linda Gail?"

There was a brief moment of silence. Suddenly, all around me, an entire classroom erupted in laughter. Kevin Perkins, at the desk across the aisle, was slapping Lee Peyton on the back. Steve Krotzer, usually quiet and studious, was practically crying.

I was horrified. Had I just said something? I couldn't remember.

Sharon Holbert and Dickie Rollins were howling, Jeff Deas was beating his desk, and Miss Wheeler was standing in the middle of it all with an open English book, looking right at me.

It was about that time when it hit me. I had called Miss Wheeler by her first name. Miss Wheeler was an adult. Miss Wheeler was my third grade teacher!

"Class!" she said loudly. "Class, calm down!" Pow! She slammed the English book to the floor. Startled into silence, we looked up at her. "I said 'calm down'," she ordered. And then, leaning down to me, she continued, "I'll see you after school."

When the final bell rang, I ducked my head and sat still as my friends left the room. I could hear them laughing in the hall as Lee Peyton did impressions of me. "What's wrong, Linda Gail? What's wrong, Linda Gail?" I wanted to hit him in the stomach.

Miss Wheeler rose from her desk. Closing the door, she walked toward me. "Andy," she began, "I think you're a wonderful young man."

*Hey, hey, hey!* I thought.

"But," she continued, "If I am to maintain control of the class, you must not call me by my first name. It seems disrespectful."

I stared at her. I didn't really understand what she was saying.

"Do you understand what I am saying?" she asked.

"Yes, ma'am," I answered.

"I know that you didn't intend to be rude," she said, "but let's be careful, okay?" And with that, she put her hand on my shoulder and said, "You are one of my favorites."

I put my hand up on her shoulder and said, "You're one of my favorites, too." Then I winked.

Walking home, I smiled as I thought of Miss Wheeler. I could tell she liked me by the way she looked at me after I winked— kind of open mouthed, blinking her eyes. So I had winked again and walked out.

Sawyerton Springs Elementary had two third grade teachers. One was Miss Wheeler, who was well liked and beautiful. The

# Wonderful Wheeler and the Flat-Out Lie

other was Mrs. Trotter.

Mrs. Trotter was short and wide. She wasn't fat—she was wide. Her eyes bulged and her red hair extended straight up from her flat forehead like fire. Mrs. Trotter waddled around the schoolyard looking for all the world like some demented troll screeching at kids. In fact, that is what we called her: Trotter the Troll.

All through second grade, we prayed to God in heaven above to reach down his mighty hand and place us in Miss Wheeler's third grade class. "In thy merciful goodness, spare us, O, Lord, from Trotter the Troll." Once, I even prayed that at the dinner table. My mother didn't think it was funny, but my dad actually squirted iced tea out his nose.

Third grade with Miss Wheeler was wonderful. Every day, after arithmetic, she would introduce "show and tell," and, because we participated alphabetically, I was always first.

As I remember, that was a good year for me. I scored big with a baby rat, a picture of Elvis, and a pair of my grandmother's underwear. They were enormous.

Normally for show and tell, one would merely produce something from a sack, but occasionally we would get permission to go into the hall and get our presentation ready. Such was the case on that particular day, and so with Kevin Perkins as my assistant, I retired to the hall. Moments later, we entered the room, each of us through a leg of those massive panties. Miss Wheeler turned a bright red, but to her credit, she never said a word.

As we returned to the hall, we were triumphant and smug in our obvious victory. Often, we were outclassed by whatever Lee Peyton brought from his father's doctor's office. Leaning against the lockers, I was about to help Kevin out of the right leg when the door adjacent to us opened. It was Mrs. Trotter.

She came fully to the middle of the hall before she saw us. Stopping suddenly, she looked, turning her head as if to adjust her vision, and then, with a croaking noise not at all unlike a giant toad, she came for us.

In an instant, both Kevin and I knew she was not coming to us—she was coming for us. So we ran. We ran down the hall as fast as we could go with Mrs. Trotter close behind. It was as if we had stolen her underwear and she was determined to get them back. "O, Lord," Kevin said, "save us from Trotter the Troll!"

We ran outside, across the play ground, and back into the other end of the school building. It was like a two-man sack race. Kevin would fall and I would fall. I would fall and Kevin would fall. We were so scared that simply getting out of the underwear never occurred to us.

Shortly, we were back where we started. Opening the door to Miss Wheeler's room, we fell inside and shut it behind us. Mrs. Trotter, seeing where we had gone, was running for the open door just as it closed. Boom! She hit it like a linebacker. As we looked up at the small window in the door, her bulging eyes rolled back in her head and Trotter the Troll slowly slid out of sight.

I found out later that Miss Wheeler had explained everything to the principal and smoothed things over with Mrs. Trotter. We never got in trouble, my parents never knew, and I was more positive than ever that Miss Wheeler was the greatest teacher in the world.

As the years passed, Miss Wheeler came through for us all many times. She remained a friend even when I wasn't in her class, but because her ultimate goal was to teach high school English, I was fortunate enough to be her student twice more as she taught different grades.

The next time I caught up with Miss Wheeler was in a seventh grade English and literature class. The assignment one week was "poetry parodies." Using poems from our literature book, we were to "make the verse our own" while maintaining the style of the original. The poems were to remain recognizable—humor was encouraged.

Still trying to impress Miss Wheeler, I chose the longest poem in the book and made a mess out of "The Wreck of the

# Wonderful Wheeler and the Flat-Out Lie

Hesperus." Lee Peyton did the best job, I thought, with his stunning adaptation of the Joyce Kilmer classic, "Trees."

> *I think that I shall never know*
> *A poem so lovely as my toe.*
> *A toe that may in summer wear*
> *Scabs from stumps everywhere.*

As the years passed, my crush on Miss Wheeler developed into an admiration for her abilities as a teacher. Her classes were taught in an atmosphere of laughter and excitement, yet she demanded respect. The day after Lee received an A for "Toes," she paddled him for calling her "Wheeler Dealer."

I was thrilled to be assigned to Miss Wheeler's English class as a senior. It was good to see that she had not changed. Our first period discussions often carried over into second period study hall, which she also supervised. Most of our class had signed up for study hall during that time, and to this day, a majority of my high school memories revolve around Miss Wheeler and those first two periods.

We talked, argued, laughed, and teased her about Coach Rainsberger, who, the year before, had taken her to our junior-senior prom wearing gym shoes with his tuxedo. I suppose, however, that there came a time when, due to familiarity, we began to see ourselves as Miss Wheeler's equal. This was not an accurate perception!

We had mistaken her interest and concern for us as an inability to see through mischief. We could have saved ourselves a zero on a major test if we'd only listened when Miss Wheeler said, "Remember, to take advantage is to invite trouble."

It was a crisp morning—not cold, but crisp. Kevin, Lee, Dickie, and I had gotten into the woods at daylight. We were squirrel hunting before school. The day had already been fantastic. Kevin and Dickie had their limits, Lee and I were one shy.

The problem we saw, as we stopped to discuss it, was time. In less than 30 minutes, first period would begin. None of us had ever gotten a limit before and now, here was a chance for all of us to accomplish that feat. But if we stayed for a limit, Dickie pointed out, we'd be late for school. And today, he warned, was the mid-term exam.

"Big deal," Kevin said, "We'll just tell Miss Wheeler we had a flat tire. You know she'll believe us. Then we can make up the test during study hall.

So that's what we did. Confidently, we strode into Miss Wheeler's room just as the second period bell rang. Looking up from her desk she asked, "Where were you?"

"We had a flat tire on my car, Miss Wheeler," Lee said. "We were down near Henley's Hardware on the back street."

She glanced at me. I nodded.

Kevin spoke. "We tried to hurry in time for the test, Miss Wheeler, but we just couldn't make it."

She glanced at me. I nodded.

"We're ready to take the test, Miss Wheeler," Dickie said. "We'll make it up right now. We'll make it up right here in study hall."

She glanced at me. I nodded.

"Okay," she agreed. "If you're ready to take the test now, let's get to it."

We tried to hide our smiles as we turned to go to our desks.

"I don't want you to sit in your regular seats," Miss Wheeler said, "I would like you each to choose one corner of the room."

As we settled into our desks, pen and paper at the ready, the greatest teacher I ever had continued. "Your make-up exam will be all essay," she said. "The essay will be the answer to only one question. And the question is. . . ." She paused. "The question is. . . Which tire was flat?"

102

What really got to Norman was the line
about the busateria service! The way he
saw it, Rick had stolen his idea.

# Store Wars

Norman's Groceteria was busier than usual this past week. Every item in the store had been marked down. Ladies crowded the aisles, browsing more than anything, sipping complimentary coffee, and talking among themselves.

By Thursday afternoon, even some of the men in town had wandered in to see if what they'd heard was true. And, after looking around a bit, they all met at the meat cooler and agreed. Yes, it seemed, Norman had priced every single item exactly three cents cheaper than Rick's Rolling Store.

Dick Rollins was holding a frozen chicken that had an X slashed over the $2.19 sticker. In red Magic Marker, it was now priced $2.16. "What'n heck started this whole thing?" he asked.

"You got me," Bubba Pratt answered. "You know Norman!" The group of men smiled and nodded.

"Oh, yeah," Tom Henley said grinning. "We know Norman!"

Walking toward the entrance, Bubba put his arm around Kevin Perkins' shoulder, opened his eyes real wide, and said, "Here we go again!"

Norman Green was born in Sawyerton Springs, but his family moved to Birmingham when he was eight. That in itself explains much of the town's reaction to Norman. "He is from here, therefore, he is one of us, but living 'up North' sure did give him a lot of weird ideas!"

Norman came back to the Springs after college and worked for several years at Henley's Hardware. By all accounts he was a successful employee. The men in town enjoyed talking to him about hunting or fishing, and consequently, they would stop in most afternoons.

Norman was especially knowledgeable about catfish, and by selling them to restaurants in nearby Foley, he made quite a bit of extra money. Every morning, he would rise before daylight to check his trotlines. Walking a good seven or eight miles in the dark between streams and ponds was nothing for Norman. He'd make it to work by 7:00, stay until 6:00 in the evening, and run his trotlines again after dark.

Day after day, every single day, Norman kept up that schedule. On Sundays, when Tom closed the hardware store, Norman went to church, and in the afternoon, he prepared his lines for the following week. No one worked harder than Norman Green.

"What's his deal?" people would ask. "He's gonna work himself to death before he's 30!"

But before too long, Norman's motives became apparent. He had a dream! He was not content to live out his life working for someone else—Norman wanted his own business.

He saved every penny that wasn't needed for immediate living expenses, and within a few years, he had quite a nest egg. It helped that Norman lived modestly and was extremely frugal. Or, as his friends put it . . . cheap.

Kevin and Bubba were in the car behind Norman one day when Norman suddenly put on the brakes, hopped out, and picked up an aluminum can he had seen beside the road. "Geez! Get a load of this, would ya," Kevin said laughing. Norman held up the can and smiled, waving as he climbed back in his car.

"That Norman is tighter'n paint on a wall," Kevin said. "When he blinks, his kneecaps move."

Bubba chuckled and shook his head. "I don't know," he said. "A guy working that hard? He'll probably own the town one day."

Well, Norman didn't want the town, but he did intend to have a piece of it. His ideas were endless and some of them had a few folks worried. For a time, he talked about opening a catfish restaurant. He was going to call it Norman's Cat House. That particular choice of names didn't go over well at the Baptist church.

"I'll put a big sign out on the bypass," Norman told Dick one morning. "It'll say, FOR A GOOD TIME, COME TO NORMAN'S CAT HOUSE . . . DOWNTOWN SAWYERTON SPRINGS! Then out to the side I'll put, CHILDREN—HALF PRICE."

Dick rolled his eyes. "Oh, brother," he said. "Here we go again."

Those four words, "here we go again," are used quite often by whomever happens to be discussing Norman at the time. His ideas have given him the reputation of one who is not so level headed as a person should be. "Or maybe," Kevin says, "he's just so far ahead of the rest of us."

For more than a year, all Norman talked about was his vision for a new chain of Jell-O stands. "They won't sell nothing but Jell-O," he'd explain. "This is an idea whose time has come! I mean, everybody knows where to go for a burger. Pizza places are everywhere, and right here in town we got Bubba's for fried chicken. So you tell me," he'd always ask smugly, "where do you go for a good bowl of Jell-O?"

Norman really had the whole thing planned out. He had drawings of what his stores would look like. He even had a menu printed that offered a variety of flavors: lime, cherry, orange, strawberry, and "specialty fruit cocktail." "The price will be the best thing," Norman said. "Fifty cents a bowl, a quarter a square, or a nickel per cube. That way, even kids can come by after school and buy a dime's worth."

"And another thing," Norman would continue, "we will only serve fresh Jell-O. Our motto will be 'If It Ain't Wiggling—We Ain't Got It!' I'll advertise the phone number so that people can call before they drive over. They'll call and ask, 'Is the Jell-O hard yet?'"

Gradually, this particular obsession of Norman's wore off. He had planned to name the chain of restaurants Jiggles and insisted that the world was ready for such a place. It became obvious, however, that Sawyerton Springs was not!

Some folks, including Miss Edna Thigpen at the *Sentinel*, felt that the name Jiggles was suggestive and that a hangout of that sort could only lead to immorality. So, when pressure came to bear, Norman backed off.

"But don't tell me it won't work," he said for weeks. "Don't even try to tell me that. It's a great idea, and someone, somewhere is gonna make millions with it. Everybody thought Einstein was a nut case, too!"

Now understand, no one really thinks Norman is a nut case, it's just that his ideas always seem to represent an uncomfortable change. That's why everyone was surprised when he decided to open a grocery store. It was . . . well, ordinary! The town needed a grocery store, that was a fact. Until Rick's Rolling Store began operations in 1973, people drove all the way to Foley for groceries.

Rick's Rolling Store was actually an old school bus. It was converted by Rick and Sue Carper into a supermarket on wheels, which literally changed the way people shopped. Suddenly, the store was at your door, allowing you the opportunity to shop conveniently.

The only catch to shopping with Rick was the selection. There's not much room on a bus—even with the added shelves and hooks—therefore, people pretty much took what they could get. It wasn't like there was a choice of frozen beans, fresh beans, dried beans, or canned beans. It was just plain beans, and a per-

# Store Wars

son felt lucky that he didn't have to drive 20 miles to get them.

Norman's grand opening was on a Saturday in August, eight years ago. He had NORMAN'S GROCETERIA written in huge letters over the front entrance, which faced College Avenue. He called it a groceteria because, as he said, "It will not only be a grocery store, it will be a cafeteria!"

Tom Henley smiled every time he said the word *groceteria.* "I knew Norman wouldn't open some regular store," he told his wife. "It's not in his nature. I saw GROCETERIA going up on that building, and I said to myself, *here we go again.*"

Well, everything was fine for years. People enjoyed the variety of Norman's, but they still appreciated the convenience of Rick's. Rick and Sue, despite the competition, never resented the groceteria, and, in fact, they ate lunch there on Mondays and Thursdays. Norman, as a professional courtesy, never charged for their meals.

Norman kept the steamer in the middle aisle, filled with the special of the day. Dessert was, of course, always Jell-O. As people filed past, they were reminded by Norman's hand lettered sign to TAKE ALL YOU WANT—EAT ALL YOU TAKE! And they did, until last Monday.

No one showed up. No one. Not even Rick and Sue! As Norman shoveled the turkey tetrazzini into freezer bags, he wondered if he'd missed something. "Was there a town picnic today or what?" he asked aloud to no one in particular. "People are buying groceries, isn't anybody eating lunch?"

Walking home after closing, Norman was still in a quandary. Why, he wondered, would his noon business all of a sudden disappear? He kicked at a piece of paper that blew across the sidewalk. Seeing the word *store* printed on the front, he picked it up. It was a business flyer:

"Are you tired of the same old lunch? Starting Monday, you can have the food you deserve delivered to your home or office. Rick's Rolling Store provides you with the same convenience you've enjoyed for years . . . now in our new busateria service!"

Well, had Norman been indoors, he would have hit the roof. He was that mad. His face darkened, his eyes narrowed, and had he not consciously remembered to breathe, he might have suffocated on the spot!

"Traitors," he muttered. He walked fast and, no longer heading home, talked to himself. "No right. They've got no right. I don't sell cloth and buttons and hammers and junk. They've got no right to serve food! Eight years I fed those people. Twice a week for eight years." Norman was boiling now. "That's more than eight hundred meals apiece!"

What really got to Norman was the line about the busateria service! The way he saw it, Rick had stolen his idea. "Groceteria, busateria," Norman said to Miss Edna Thigpen, "It's too close for coincidence. Don't tell me the man thought of it himself!"

Norman had walked straight to Miss Edna Thigpen's house on Keating Drive and was now sitting in her living room. Miss Edna, the owner and editor of the *Sawyerton Springs Sentinel*, was about to make the biggest advertising sale in the history of the newspaper.

"I've got Rick's price list at home," Norman said. "I'll bring it over tomorrow. I want a full-page ad. On the top left, have it say "Rick's Prices" and list every single item in a column underneath. At the top right, in big letters, I want "NORMAN'S PRICES!" Underneath, I want each corresponding item marked three cents less.

Norman paid Miss Edna for the ad right there. But before he stalked out of her house, he included one final item. "At the bottom of the page, in the biggest letters of all," he directed, "put this: 'CALL FOR OUR NEW LUNCH DELIVERY!'"

When the *Sentinel* came out, Rick knew that he was at war, but after all, he had fired the first shot. Rick lowered his prices. Norman lowered his. Then Rick again. Then Norman. Soon they were giving things away. There's no telling where the whole thing might have gone had it not been for Sue.

# Store Wars

Just yesterday, she hauled Rick to Norman's. She got Norman out of his office, and in front of everyone she said, "You're both acting like kids. You're killing each other off, and the town is laughing at us. I am no longer participating in this fiasco. Rick, I don't know where you'll get your meals for the bus to deliver, but I'm not cooking them! I hate to cook. Why do you think I've eaten at Norman's for eight years?"

Rick started to say something, but withering him with a look, Sue continued. "So this is what we're going to do," she said. "Rick, we will still deliver lunches to anyone in town who wants them. Norman, they will be your lunches. That way, you will both increase your business, and I don't have to cook. Everybody wins. You've been friends too long to let something this stupid come between you."

For a moment, there was silence. Then, slowly, the two men looked at each other and smiled. "That's a great idea," Norman said. "Rick, I don't know why we didn't think of this years ago. We could expand this same concept into other towns. Maybe get a fleet of buses to deliver with. Can you put a refrigerator on one of those things? Jell-O has to be cool, you know. And something else we can try. . . ."

As he listened to Norman, Rick put his arm around Sue, gave her a squeeze, and in her ear he whispered, "Here we go again!"

*Mr. Michael Ted liked Elvis Presley. No,
strike that. Mr. Michael Ted loved
Elvis Presley.*

# Mr. Michael Ted's Big Production

M ichael Ted Williams passed away last week. He was 94. He was tall and skinny and had been a part of the landscape in Sawyerton Springs for as long as anyone could remember. When I was a kid, we often stopped by Mr. Michael Ted's house after school. He was old then, but you'd never have known it. Always laughing, he lived alone in a big, two-story house off Cherokee Avenue—just him and his cats.

Mr. Michael Ted had more than 10,000 cats, or at least it seemed that way. There were cats inside the house, outside the house, around the house, and on the house. He had black cats, white cats, and every kind of cat in between. Funny thing though, he actually claimed to hate cats.

"You give me a wet cat and a good kick," he'd say, "and I'll get forty yards out of one of them things! Sneaky jerks—communist is what they are. Always peeking around corners, spying on everybody. They're the rear ends of the animal world!"

"Well, why do you keep them?" we'd ask.

"I can't get 'em to leave," he'd fume. "I tell 'em to get lost every day, but they stay around to torture me. Don't ever try to tell a cat nothing, kid, because he ain't gonna listen."

For all the talking Michael Ted Williams did about hating the cats, he never adequately explained to anyone why he bought 50-pound sacks of cat food. Or why he made toys for them. Or why he made them all sleep inside when it was cold.

There was one place in his house, however, where the cats were not allowed. It was an area the whole town knew about, because most of us had been through it. We younger people thought it was neat, but it's very existence caused most of the adults in town to think Michael Ted Williams was rather a nut. I am referring to the Elvis Room.

Mr. Michael Ted liked Elvis Presley. No, strike that. Mr. Michael Ted *loved* Elvis Presley. He absolutely idolized the man.

It seemed strange to us that an older person would be so crazy about an entertainer like Elvis, but he was. "Bing Crosby and them guys ain't got a clue," he'd say. "Elvis does it all. He can sing, he can act, and he loved his mother."

The Elvis Room was at the end of the hall on the second floor. It was a shrine. Hundreds of pictures were stacked on shelves anchored by Elvis decanters or other figurines. Movie posters were on the walls—*Fun in Acapulco*, *Girls, Girls, Girls*, *Viva Las Vegas*, *G. I. Blues*, and *Clambake*—all framed nicely.

By the door, a filing cabinet held all of Elvis' single records, which were still in their original jackets. One hundred twenty-nine ticket stubs were neatly displayed on a table in the corner. Each stub was a reminder of a particular concert attended by Mr. Michael Ted.

# Mr. Michael Ted's Big Production

"That there's the scarf Elvis wore in Louisville," he would say as he showed someone through the room. "Real sweat on it, too. See that stain? Here's a popcorn bag from Tallahassee. Somebody threw it on stage. Elvis kicked it off, and I caught it. I was right there—right in the first row."

Every now and then, one of the kids in town would say something mean about Elvis just to get a rise out of Mr. Michael Ted. It always worked. Once, Jeff Deas made a comment about prescription medicine and, I believe, actually used the term *druggie* before finding his left ear wrapped around the old man's index finger.

Elvis had migraines, Jeff was told, and suffered from several old karate injuries. And unless Jeff wanted to know first-hand how a karate injury felt, he was to keep his opinions about pharmaceuticals to himself!

When Elvis died in 1977, Mr. Michael Ted left his cats in the care of his nephew Billy Pat and headed to Memphis. We saw him drive out of town past the elementary school with tears rolling down his face. For three days, he stood outside the gates at Graceland, paying his respects with thousands of others.

He met a lady about his same age, Patsy Jones, from DeKalb, Mississippi. She had met Elvis once at a train station. Having missed her connection that night, she hadn't had any money to eat supper. Patsy showed Mr. Michael Ted the $5 bill Elvis had given her for food, and as he held the bill admiringly, he asked why she hadn't spent it. She had been too excited to eat she told him, and besides, she added, it was the nicest thing anyone had ever done for her.

When he got back to town, there wasn't a trace of sadness in Michael Ted Williams. "Elvis was way too young to go," he explained, "but the young fellow had a good life. He helped a lot of people ease their loneliness, and I, for one, will always be grateful. We still got his music . . . so we still got him."

From that point until his own passing last week, Mr. Michael Ted actually increased his obsession with Elvis, but in a happy way. He would travel hundreds of miles to talk to someone who knew the singer, he bought and traded more memorabilia, and even held an Elvis dance every spring for the high school. Nothing but Elvis songs were played for the kids, who were all dressed like Elvis and Priscilla. Priscilla was, according to Mr. Michael Ted, the only woman Elvis ever really loved.

About a year ago, Mr. Michael Ted started giving away his cats. "I ain't real young anymore y'know, and these fur balls need to be kicked around by somebody." Almost every person in town took a cat or two. We knew that he was preparing for the end. What we didn't know, however, was how prepared he actually was!

"I'll be stopping by the bank on the way in to work," Billy Pat said to his wife, Ginny, at breakfast Wednesday morning. "Everything is already set, I think, but the will said that the funeral instructions were in a safety deposit box." As the closest blood relation to the deceased, Billy Pat Williams had been named executor of the estate.

It was all very simple actually. The house and lot were to become the property of the Methodist Church. The contents of the house were to be divided between friends and family, except for the Elvis memorabilia. It was all to be carefully packed and shipped to DeKalb, Mississippi, in care of a Patsy Jones.

Billy Pat arrived at the bank shortly after they opened and followed a teller into the vault. He unlocked box number 30024, and inside he found an envelope marked: INSTRUCTIONS. Slipping it into his jacket pocket, Billy Pat thanked the teller, left the bank, and drove directly to the only funeral home in Sawyerton Springs, Max's Mortuary.

Max Reed, the mortician, met Billy Pat in the foyer, took the unopened envelope, and assured him that all would be taken care of. "I'll call you after lunch with the final details," Max said, "but let's go ahead and set the service for Friday at 2 p.m."

Ten minutes later, as Billy Pat walked into his office, his secretary held the phone out to him and said, "Mr. Reed is on the phone. It must be important, because he insisted on holding, and he has been holding for seven or eight minutes!"

Billy Pat wrinkled his eyebrows in a confused manner and took the phone. "Yeah, Max, this is Billy Pat. What's going on?"

"Billy Pat? Did you read the instructions your uncle left for his funeral?" Max asked.

"Well, no," Billy Pat said, "I never even opened the envelope."

Max continued. "Did he, by chance, ever give you any idea of his plans?"

"No, I don't think so."

"Did Mr. Michael Ted's will say anything about the funeral?"

"Just that his instructions were to be followed," Billy Pat said. "What's this all about anyway?"

"It's about the biggest send-off this town has ever had. Or is likely to ever have. For God's sake, Billy Pat, get down here—you ain't gonna believe this!"

On Friday afternoon at 2:00, Beauman's Pond United Methodist Church was filled to overflowing. In fact, I believe it safe to say that the entire town was there. Every man, woman, and child— even some people who weren't particularly close to Mr. Michael Ted. There existed an air of expectation one rarely experiences at a funeral.

Near the casket were rows and rows of flowers. Gorgeous sprays of carnations and roses surrounded sayings like "Gone, But Not Forgotten" or "In Our Hearts Forever." Near the steps of the church's pulpit was the arrangement from Miss Luna Myers and Miss Edna Thigpen. It was a plastic telephone encircled by purple gladiolas and white mums. Above the phone were the words: *Jesus Called—Michael Ted Answered.*

Max Reed stood to the side. He was horrified. He knew what was about to come, and it seemed to him almost indecent, but he had done exactly as the man requested.

Pastor Wade Ward sat in his chair on the pulpit. Crossing and uncrossing his legs constantly, he kept wiping his face with a handkerchief. Pastor Ward was nervous. Maybe it was the music. "Love Me Tender" was playing in the background. New things always made Pastor Ward nervous, and today, he was about to perform his first Elvis funeral.

Max nodded at Terri Henley who approached the pulpit to sing a song. *This is nuts*, she thought, *A song like this at a funeral? Well, here goes. . . .*

"You aren't anything but a hound dog, crying all the time. You aren't anything but a hound dog, crying all the time. You haven't ever caught a rabbit, and you aren't any friend of mine."

Terri sang the song. She wasn't happy about it, but she did it. It wasn't appropriate to use improper English in church, she felt, so she took the liberty of changing some words. "Well, they said you were high class, but that was not the truth. . . ."

She also sang "Heartbreak Hotel" and "Teddy Bear." Several people snickered when she finished her last song and said, "Thank you. Thank you very much."

Then it was Pastor Ward's turn. "Brothers and sisters," he began, "We are gathered here to mourn the loss of a friend. He was a very unusual man." Pastor Ward said later that that was the only occasion in his ministry when the whole congregation "amened" a single statement. As he finished his prepared words about how wonderful a person the deceased had been, Pastor Ward paused to say a silent prayer of his own. "Dear God," he muttered, "Get me through this next part."

Reading from a printed sheet of paper Max had given to him earlier, Pastor Ward said, "And now, ladies and gentlemen . . . the moment you've all been waiting for . . . from Sawyerton Springs, Alabama . . . Michael Ted Williams."

Max Reed pushed the button on a tape player and started toward the coffin.

BAHHHHHHHHHHHHHHHM. BAHHHHHHHHHHHHHHM. BAHHHHHHHHHHHHHHHM. BAH DAHMMMMMMM! BAHM

# Mr. Michael Ted's Big Production

PAHM, BAHM PAHM, BAHM PAHM, BAHM PAHM, BAHMMM-MMMMMMMMM. . . .

As the music from *2001 . . . A Space Odyssey* filled the sanctuary, Max slowly lifted the casket lid.

. . . BAH DAH DAH, DAH, DAH DAH DAH! DAH DAH DAH, DAH, DAH, DAH!

As the lid opened, the mourners (if indeed they could have been called that) stood up and moved forward to get a better look. At the loudest part of the song, Max had the casket fully open, and, as he stepped back, people broke into applause.

There, amid the flash bulbs popping was Michael Ted Williams. His hair had been dyed jet black. He was wearing fake sideburns and a gold tux. He looked good. In fact, that's exactly what everyone said. "Doesn't he look good?" He didn't look natural, but a few people said so anyway. Everyone did agree, however, that he looked exactly as he had intended. He looked like a 94-year-old Elvis!

It is an understatement to say that no one will ever forget Mr. Michael Ted. He was a great old guy who provided us with laughter even after his passing. One can imagine him chuckling as he wrote down the instructions for his own funeral—the most amazing production any of us had ever seen.

There was one more time during the service in which the congregation applauded. It was out of respect and admiration for the old man. Applause is intended as acknowledgement of a job well done, whether that job is a show or life itself. So the congregation stood as one, clapping and cheering, as the casket was carried out of the church.

And then, with a big smile on his face, Pastor Ward looked at the people and said, "Ladies and gentlemen, you can all go home. Michael Ted has left the building!"

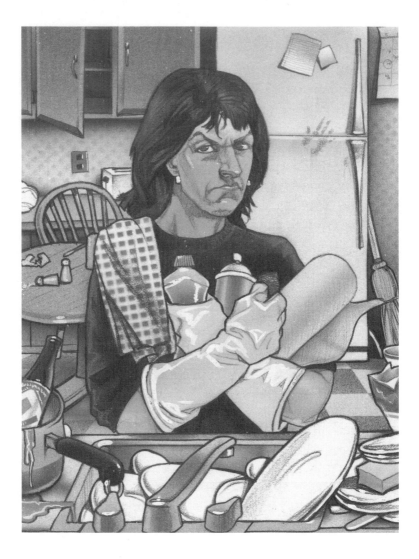

"Boy oh boy," Ginny said out loud, "if he were here, I'd tell him what he could do with that meeting. And the shirt!"

# The Secret War of Ginny Williams

Ginny Williams was mad. In fact, she couldn't remember being quite so mad. It was just after 8:00 in the morning and she already had a headache. Sitting at the breakfast table in her pink bathrobe, she held her coffee cup with both hands to avoid spilling the hot liquid. Ginny was shaking. Ginny was mad.

Billy Pat, Ginny's husband, had pulled out of the driveway only moments before. "Don't forget my white shirt," he said as he walked out the door. "I'll need it tomorrow. And I can't meet you for lunch today—got a meeting with Bubba Pratt. Anything you need me to do?" She shook her head. "Okay then," he said, oblivious to her growing anger, "I love ya." He got in his car and drove away.

Ginny didn't answer until Billy Pat was around the corner.

"Yeah, right," she said and went inside. Pouring coffee into her cup and all over the counter, she replayed in her mind exactly what Billy Pat had said.

"Don't forget my white shirt." *How can I forget it,* Ginny thought, *you leave it in the middle of the bedroom floor. If I forgot it, I'd trip and break my neck. That's what I should have said. That would've been good. And why can't you meet me for lunch is what I ought to have told him. Thursday is supposed to be our day for lunch. Is meat loaf at the cafe once a week too much to ask? Yeah, well, you always have a meeting with Bubba Pratt. I don't care if you have a meeting with the president of the United States, I'm your wife. That's supposed to count for something.*

"Boy oh boy," Ginny said out loud, "if he were here, I'd tell him what he could do with that meeting. And the shirt!"

She pushed her chair back and stood up to begin cleaning away the breakfast dishes. As she balanced the cereal bowls for the move toward the sink, the top one fell, sending a shower of milk and glass all over the kitchen.

The word Ginny selected at that moment was not one with which she was totally unfamiliar. In fact, she had grounded her youngest daughter for saying the same thing just last week. But somehow, when Ginny said the word, it was satisfying—rolling, as it did, crisp and clean from her lips. The word also perfectly described her mood.

Cleaning up the mess, Ginny tried to remember what else Billy Pat had said. What was it? Her eyes narrowed. She remembered. He had said, "Anything you need me to do?"

*Yeah, there's something I need you to do,* she thought. *There's quite a few things I need you to do. Starting with getting the garbage out on time. Mondays and Thursdays. The garbage goes out on Mondays and Thursdays just like it has around here for the last 500 years. So that's one thing you can do. Remember the garbage.*

*And how about not asking me 20 times "what's for supper?" I'll cook it—you eat it, okay? Mow the lawn more than once a month would be a good one. That way, maybe the neighbors won't think we're growing hay.*

As Ginny showered and dressed, she knew that what made her most angry was the fact that at that very moment, wherever Billy Pat was, he had no idea that she was even upset! In a way, it made her feel better to think of the things she would say if he were standing in front of her.

*Lose some weight. How about that, fatso? Or, maybe you're going to start a Sawyerton Springs Sumo Wrestling League?* Ginny smiled. That would have gotten him. Billy Pat had gained 15 pounds since Christmas, and he was pretty sensitive about it.

*You might stop snoring. That's something you could do. Also, don't mess with the thermostat after I've set it, quit belching at the table, and for once in your life, could you put the toilet seat down?*

The phone rang. It was Glenda Perkins. Could she, she wanted to know, borrow Ginny's toaster? Glenda was having company and wanted to fix a nice breakfast the next morning. They didn't have a toaster, she explained, because Kevin felt that the oven did an adequate job, and he didn't want to spend money on a luxury item like that.

Ginny wrapped the electrical cord around the toaster as she walked to her car. She had to deliver the appliance to Glenda because Kevin wouldn't spring for a second vehicle either. Fastening her seat belt, Ginny said aloud, "At least Billy Pat isn't cheap."

As she drove to the Perkins house, she remembered the time she had mentioned to Billy Pat that their bed had been bothering her back. When they went to look at mattresses, he ended up buying her the bedroom suite she'd always wanted. "The best wife in the world deserves fine furniture," he had said. She found out later that he used money he had been saving for a fishing boat.

Ginny visited with Glenda for a couple of hours, then went to lunch alone. Thursday was her day for eating out, and she was determined not to miss it. She did, however, go to Norman's

Groceteria in order to avoid Billy Pat at the cafe.

She sat at the corner table and ate macaroni and cheese with a salad. For dessert she had lime Jell-O. Ginny had spoken to Norman when she arrived, but the place was relatively empty, so there was plenty of time to sit and think.

*Why do I have to eat alone*, she wondered. *It's not fair. He's always working—or says he is. Is one lunch a week too much to ask? He doesn't seem to care. Heck, he doesn't even know I'm mad.*

Ginny thought back to the night, 21 years earlier, when Billy Pat had proposed. He had been 40 minutes late picking her up at her house, and she was furious. She didn't even speak to him until they were in the car. "I have been waiting forever," she had said.

"I'm sorry," he replied. "Work, y'know."

"Yeah, I know," she said, "All you think about is work. Ever since you got this new job, you live and breathe work. It's gotten to be the most important thing in your life."

Suddenly, she remembered, Billy Pat had swerved the car to the side of the road and stopped. Now, he was mad. "Look here," he had told her, "It's not the most important thing in my life, but it'll allow me to do the most important thing in my life. This afternoon, when I asked your dad if I could marry you, I told him I would take care of you. I don't have a desire to work hard, I have a responsibility. That's different. I love you. This ring is for you."

Ginny had listened to him with her mouth open, tears rolling down her cheeks. "I love you, too" was all she could say. "I love you, too."

Sitting there in Norman's, Ginny wiped her eyes and blew her nose. *It's different now, she reasoned. We aren't kids anymore. Billy Pat owns his own business, a very successful one, and he doesn't need to spend the time with it that he does. It is different, isn't it?*

Ginny paid her check and left. She didn't talk to Norman on the way out. He had seemed kind of touchy earlier when she made a joke about the price war he and Rick Carper had been through. He didn't even smile. *I'm glad Billy Pat can take a joke*, she thought.

# The Secret War of Ginny Williams

Ginny laughed out loud remembering her husband's picture on the front page of the *Sentinel*. Billy Pat had shot up a living room with a .22 rifle trying to kill a flying squirrel. It didn't appear that anyone in town would ever forget the incident. Billy Pat had heard enough jokes about Rambo to last a lifetime, but he chuckled at them all.

Then there was the time when she and Billy Pat had been playing Scrabble. The score was close and the game was coming to an end when Billy Pat stood up and aggressively challenged the word *suit*. "*Su it?*" he demanded. "What kind of word is *su it?*" That had been years ago, and they still laughed about it!

When Ginny got home, she flipped on the television. "Soap operas," she grumbled. "I hate soap operas." Just the same, she sat down and watched.

For the next three hours, Ginny counted 34 different people having affairs. As she turned the set off, she was glad that she didn't have that kind of thing to worry about. Billy Pat, she knew, was not that kind of man.

Ginny was about to start planning supper when Bonnie Pat, Janine, and Janelle burst through the door. The three teenagers kissed their mother and introduced her to a friend of theirs from school. Ginny recognized the girl as Robert and Cindy Wainright's daughter. Robert, her father, spent all his time hunting and fishing. Ginny had never seen him with his daughter.

*I hope our girls know how lucky they are,* Ginny thought. *Billy Pat's a great dad.*

Billy Pat had never seemed disappointed that he had no sons. He coached his daughters' softball teams, chaperoned their classes on field trips, and as they each turned 15, he insisted on being their first date.

Ginny puttered around the kitchen as she remembered Billy Pat giving the girls a corsage and taking them all the way to Foley for dinner. He held the doors as they walked through and even ordered for them at the Shrimp Boat, the nicest restaurant in town. He wanted the girls to expect the best from the boys they would be dating, and Billy Pat wanted to be the standard by which those boys were measured.

Lost in her thoughts, Ginny jumped when the doorbell rang. Opening the front door, she saw the florist truck drive away. There, on the porch, were a dozen red roses. *They must be for Bonnie Pat*, she thought. The Henley boy had been sending flowers a lot lately. Bending down to pick up the vase, she saw the envelope attached to the roses. The envelope had her name on it.

She brought the roses inside and sat down on the floor next to the couch. With the vase between her knees, Ginny opened the envelope and pulled out the card. In Billy Pat's handwriting, it read: "Lunch today was no fun. Bubba is not nearly as pretty as you. I'm lucky to have a wife who is so understanding. I can't wait to see you tonight. I miss you. I love you. Billy Pat."

*I was right*, Ginny thought, as she put the flowers in their bedroom. *He didn't even know I was angry.*

And she was glad.

"Get the net," Billy Pat screamed as he reeled frantically. "She'll go 11 pounds easy. Hurry up."

# Billy Pat, Dick, and Gilligan, Too

For a moment, it looked as if he was about to be killed. Backed up against the red ice chest in the bow of the aluminum boat, he picked up a paddle to defend himself. Dick Rollins knew he deserved to die for what he'd done. And for that reason, he almost put the paddle down.

Fearfully, he glanced behind him, searching for an escape. There was none—he was trapped. There was no help within a half-mile. Dick was all alone on the backwaters of Beauman's Pond. All alone in a 12-foot boat with his former best friend, Billy Pat Williams, who was now about to end his life.

Only seconds earlier, Billy Pat had been a happy man. Casting a big purple worm with his brand new rod and reel, he set the hook on the fish of a lifetime. Both Dick and Billy Pat watched open mouthed as the huge bass jumped clear of the water. "Ten pounds," Dick said breathlessly. "That bass'll weigh 10 pounds."

"Get the net," Billy Pat screamed as he reeled frantically. Dick scrambled into the bottom of the boat and retrieved the landing net just as Billy Pat guided the fish alongside.

"My God," Billy Pat croaked. "She'll go 11 easy. Hurry up, Dick!"

As Dick extended the net, the trophy jumped again right at the boat. Surprised, Dick made a swipe for the fish . . . and knocked it off the line. As the bass slowly swam away, Billy Pat made a move as if he were about to dive in after it, but turned toward Dick instead.

Dick actually felt nauseated. Had he done something minor, like burning down Billy Pat's house or wrecking his car, all would have been forgiven. But this was not the case. What he had done was unpardonable.

Billy Pat's eyes were wild as he stumbled over the center seat. "You did that on purpose!" he yelled. Moving toward Dick, Billy Pat stepped on Dick's rod, breaking it in two. "And," he said, "I did that on purpose!"

By this time, Dick had backed up as far as he possibly could and was actually leaning out over the water. Wielding the paddle in front of him again, he said, "You're crazy, Billy Pat. You know I didn't mean to lose that fish! Now, get away from me or you're gonna turn this boat over!"

"How'd you know I was gonna turn that boat over?" Billy Pat asked Dick as they sat on an island in the middle of the swamp.

Dick glared at him. "Any idiot coulda seen it was fixin' to happen, you dumbutt! Of all the stupid things anybody ever did . . . geez!"

Both men were soaked and miserable. When the boat tilted, water had come over the side, and the craft literally sank from under them. Luckily, they had been near a small strip of land when the accident occurred, and that is where they ended up. Billy Pat had saved only his tackle box. Dick still clutched the paddle.

# Billy Pat, Dick, and Gilligan, Too

"Are you still mad?" Billy Pat asked.

"No," Dick answered.

"You still look mad."

"Well, I'm not."

"If you're not mad, then how come that vein on your neck is sticking out?"

"If you don't shut up, I'm gonna get mad!"

Both Dick and Billy Pat blamed each other for the situation in which they found themselves. Dick's view was that Billy Pat had lost control of himself and sunk the boat. Billy Pat, on the other hand, was of the opinion that had Dick not lost his fish in the first place, he wouldn't have lost control.

"So, what do we do now?" Billy Pat wondered aloud.

"I don't know," Dick answered. "It's too far to swim, that's for sure. And it's gonna be dark in an hour."

The swamp is located on the eastern side of Sawyerton Springs, on the far end of Beauman's Pond. Fed by the springs, it is more of a wooded lake than a swamp. The water there is deep and clear. Cypress trees and water oaks draped with Spanish moss give the swamp an isolated feeling and, in fact, it is rather isolated. Stretching for several miles, the backwater is broken up only by a few small areas of high ground—most of which are less than 15 to 20 yards long. It was one of these islands on which the two men were stranded.

Dick and Billy Pat, best friends and neighbors, have fished together every Saturday for years. It was only last month that they decided to go in partners and buy the boat that now sat at the bottom of the swamp. It had been outfitted with a ten horsepower motor, two anchors, the works.

"I sure am glad you insisted on those extra large anchors," Billy Pat said dryly.

"Yeah," Dick answered, "the whole rig did seem to sink a lot faster."

"What time you reckon they'll miss us?" Billy Pat asked.

131

"Soon, I hope," Dick said. "I'm supposed to take Kathy to Foley tonight."

"Gettin' dark," Billy Pat said. "Did you tell anybody where we'd be fishing?"

"Nope."

"Me, neither."

Suddenly, Billy Pat remembered the tackle box. He had put waterproof matches in one of the drawers years ago for just such an emergency. He quickly found them as Dick broke the paddle up to burn. A signal fire was just what they needed.

Unfortunately, wet paddles are usually difficult to light, and this one was no exception. Billy Pat held match after match on the soaked wood until each in turn burned his fingers and was dropped. Finally, only one match was left.

"Here," Billy Pat said, "You light this one. I've got some reel cleaning fluid in my tackle box. I'll pour it on the wood when you strike it. Maybe that'll help."

"Is it flammable?" Dick asked.

Unscrewing the cap, Billy Pat replied, "I think so."

As it turned out, "flammable" was a rather weak description of the reaction of the fluid on the flaming match. Dick heard a loud "whomp!"

Everything was on fire. The island was on fire. The air was on fire. Even the water was on fire. Fortunately, the pair had on extremely wet clothes. Neither Dick nor Billy Pat could recall later whether they had jumped at the explosion or were actually blown into the air, but both agreed that the mushroom cloud was probably a first for Sawyerton Springs.

"You look kinda strange without eyebrows," Billy Pat said. Things had settled down again and the paddle was now the only thing burning. "I wish I had some marshmallows. You hungry?"

"No."

"I am."

Billy Pat tried to keep the conversation going. He was in a hole

# Billy Pat, Dick, and Gilligan, Too

now and he knew it. For a while there, what with the netting incident and all, Dick had been feeling pretty low. His smugness was returning, however, as the moron scales tilted toward Billy Pat. Both were aware that a boat sinking and an explosion beat a lost bass any day of the week.

"Remember how many snakes we used to see on these islands?" Billy Pat asked.

"No, actually I had forgotten that," Dick said, "but thank you very much for reminding me."

"Billy Pat looked thoughtful, then said, "Guess this is probably what Gilligan felt like."

Dick glanced sideways. "What?" he said.

"Gilligan," Billy Pat explained. "You know. Gilligan . . . on 'Gilligan's Island.' They were castaways and we're kind of castaways, and I'll bet this is how he felt."

Dick stared at Billy Pat.

Billy Pat continued. "Did you ever wonder where they got all those clothes? I mean, it was just a three-hour tour. Why would anybody have that many clothes on a three-hour tour?"

"I wish I had some clothes," Dick mumbled. "My pants are wet, my shirt is burned . . . that whole deal was really stupid, y'know?"

"I know," Billy Pat said. "It was stupid. Like, why couldn't they get off that island? Here's the Professor—a guy who could build a radio out of coconuts and sticks—he couldn't build a boat?"

"I wish somebody'd build me a boat," Dick said.

"And another thing," Billy Pat wondered, "What was Gilligan's last name?"

"Who cares?"

"No, seriously, think about it. They never said! Was it Gilligan Smith? Or Gilligan Poindexter?"

Dick, in an effort to quiet Billy Pat, said, "Look. It was just Gilligan, okay? It was just plain Gilligan."

After a moment of silence, Billy Pat said, "Yeah, I see. You're probably right. It was just plain Gilligan . . . like Charo or Cher."

Dick rolled his eyes. "Will you shut up?" Then listening closely, he whispered, "I think I hear a boat." He stood up, but after several minutes said, "Well, no, I guess not. Sorry."

"That's all right. Mary Ann and Ginger always thought they were hearing boats, too. By the way, I'm sorry I sunk ours."

"Well," Dick said, smiling. "I'm sorry I lost your fish. She probably would have pushed 12 or 13 pounds."

"No problem," Billy Pat said, chuckling. "Maybe you'll hook her next time, and I can knock her off for you!"

Dick laughed. "By the way, how're we gonna get off of here? You haven't got a radio do ya?"

"I ain't even got a coconut," Billy Pat said, grinning. "Hey! Did Gilligan ever get off his island?"

"I don't know," Dick said. He wrinkled his brow. "Seems like the show just ended and we never found out."

"That's what I thought," Billy Pat said. "After all that time, they just come to the end and don't tell you anything. Did they get off the island? Did they not get off the island? Geez, I hate to be left hanging!"

"C'mon, kid, you can do it," the man kept
telling me, "a little girl just did."

# Unfair Tales of Midway Madness

The 94th annual Kemper County Fair closed its gates late Saturday night after a successful week. Tom Henley, for one, was glad it was over. "Good gosh-a-mighty," he exclaimed to Billy Pat Williams, "you'd a thought we had the only fair in the world the way people crowd in here."

Billy Pat agreed. As this years' co-chair of the event, it was his duty to oversee the parking situation at the fairgrounds, which was, as he put it, "a job and a half." For the first time ever, the steering committee had decided not to charge three dollars per vehicle, as had been done in the past, but to assess one dollar for every person in the vehicle.

This, everyone felt, was a much more responsible method of admission. It not only made sense financially, it would end the teenagers' attempts to pack 10 to 12 kids in a single car.

By all accounts, the new parking rules were a success. Billy Pat thought so because it all ran smoothly; the committee thought so because receipts were up 17 percent; and the teenagers thought so because eight kids can fit in the trunk of an Oldsmobile.

The fairgrounds are actually just a big field running parallel to Highway 59 outside of Sawyerton Springs. Parking is, of course, just off the highway, with the main gate immediately beyond that. The livestock tents have traditionally circled the midway, giving city people the "aroma" of what a county fair is supposed to be in the first place.

Intermingled with the livestock tents were the craft, home goods, and school science tents. An additional tent was used this year for local merchants to display and sell their wares.

On Tuesday, judging was held in the home goods competition. Jan Jones won first place for her tomatoes and green beans, Glenda Perkins took a first with her ginger snap cookies, and for the eleventh year in a row, Best in Show was given to the same person: Annirae Edwards. She won in the pickle division with a recipe calling for a hint of allspice. The recipe was given to her, she said, by her mother, Clara, who lives in North Carolina.

The area schools did a wonderful job with the science tent and their theme: "The Future Is Ahead of Us!" Two hundred eggs in one booth were being hatched by an electric blanket, and a corner of the tent was dedicated to showing us how we will shop in the future by using our televisions. The sign, made of Elmer's Glue and red glitter, proclaimed: INTERACTIVE TV—ARE YOU READY?

The big hit of the science tent, however, was reserved for the Henley boy. Only a junior in high school, Tommy made a water-powered lawn mower. Hooked to a garden hose, it would cut the grass and water it at the same time. Besides having his picture in the *Sentinel*, he won a fifty dollar gift certificate at Norman's Groceteria.

The Future Farmers of America, in conjunction with the 4-H Club, competed for trophies and ribbons on Wednesday. Cows, horses, sheep, pigs, goats, chickens, and even rabbits were available for viewing.

The auction on Thursday was lively, and more than a few animals were purchased by parents of the children who raised them. This is a yearly phenomenon. It makes no difference how often Mom or Dad said, "You know, of course, what cows are for. . . ." or "That's the part where we get bacon. . . ." When the man from the meat-packing plant is bidding on old Lulu, a sobbing child often prompts a parent to reach for the wallet.

While the tent for local merchants was enthusiastically accepted by the local merchants, most of the fairgoers gave it mixed reviews. Miss Edna Thigpen of the *Sentinel* wrote, "Why should we go to a fair to see Norman's groceries in a booth? If I want to see one of Billy Pat's foreign cars, I'll go to his car lot! Henley's Hardware with a display of hammers and screwdrivers? Who cares? And what is Max Reed thinking about?"

Actually, quite a few people wondered what Max Reed was thinking about. Max, of Max's Mortuary, had a rather large selection of coffins and tombstones on display. Most people stared for a moment, blinked, and hurried on past. Bubba Pratt, with his fried chicken stand right next to Max, was furious: "He's killing everyone's business, no pun intended. This is a fair for gosh sake, what does he think people are gonna do? Does he think people are gonna say, 'Well, heck, honey. While we're here, let's go ahead and buy a casket.' Geez!"

With the exception of the local merchant's tent, very little has changed or is new since I was a boy. The Kemper County Fair started in 1899 as a time for farmers and their families to get together for a week and celebrate the harvest. Only years later were midway rides and attractions added.

When I was an eighth grader, the rides and attractions *were* the fair. And there was something about the people who ran the rides and attractions that provided an element of danger to life in a small town.

Fair week was the only week during the year when people in Sawyerton Springs locked their doors. The roustabouts and carneys were thrust at us as an example of what could happen to our lives if we didn't do our homework. "Look at that child," our parents would say, "how'd you like to have that many mosquito bites on your legs?"

Often, being hurried down the midway, someone was pointed out as the product of an illspent youth: "You could end up with a job like that if you don't watch it."

To my way of thinking, "a job like that" didn't seem half bad. I even practiced what I heard one man saying. I had it down. The gravelly monotone sounded good. I'd sit with my legs crossed at the knees, hunch up my shoulders and say, "She's right behind this curtain, friends. She's waiting just for you. She's inside, and she's alive—Nina the headless girl. A freak of nature, the good Lord's only mistake—Nina, the headless girl. Ladies and gentlemen, boys and girls, one thin dime will buy your time—Nina, the headless girl."

Over and over I'd do it—just like the man on the midway had. The last time I did that particular bit was the first time my father heard it. Actually, there was no one in the church at the time, and I still think the microphone made it sound great.

The fair of my eighth grade year was special. It was the first time I was to be allowed freedom on the midway—no adults. Kevin Perkins, Lee Peyton, and I would have run of the place. We each had five dollars we had saved for the express purpose of blowing at the fair.

Our plan was to budget a small amount for food and use the rest for the important stuff. No rides. Heck, our parents let us get on the rides! We wanted to taste the forbidden fruit—sideshows and the games!

None of us had ever been permitted to enter a sideshow, and we could only wonder why. Lee said it was because of "nakedness." "Sure, Nina ain't got no head," he said slyly, "but I'll betcha she's got everything else!"

The games, on the other hand, were forbidden for an entirely different reason. They were impossible. "You can't win," my father told me over and over. "The people you see carrying stuffed animals around are plants. Are any of your friends loaded down with prizes? No. Because you can't win."

*What does it take*, I would think, *to knock over some milk bottles with a baseball? How could you not pop a balloon with a dart? I could do it. I would do it.*

On Friday night, after eating several corn dogs each, we headed through the horse tent to the midway. There, grooming her barrel racer, was our English teacher from the year before. "Hi, Miss Wheeler," we said as we passed. "We're going to get you a teddy bear."

She smiled and said, "Thanks, guys. I appreciate it, but I already have a teddy bear, and besides, the way those games are set up, you can't win."

With that in and out of our minds, we continued on. We checked things out for about 30 minutes, then regrouped near the pig tent to discuss our options.

"Well, I'm definitely knockin' over them milk bottles," I said. "What'r you guys gonna win at?"

"Darts for me," Kevin said, "I guess I'll get my mom that stuffed snake."

"Aren't we gonna see any sideshows?" Lee asked. "I'd kinda like to see Larry the Lizard Boy."

So that was first on the agenda. Larry the Lizard Boy turned out not to be so much a boy as a full-grown man. And, we agreed, Miss Trotter in the third grade had a skin condition much worse than Larry's.

We also saw Benjamin Franklin's brain in a jar and Sam Spaniel, the man with a face like a dog. But the best was Sheba . . . Jungle Queen—raised by gorillas, captured by scientists.

Sheba growled, jumped around her cage, and ate with her

hands. Later, we saw her eating at the Band Boosters Hamburger Stand with Larry the Lizard Boy. She was still eating with her hands.

Though I had almost three dollars left, I had only budgeted one dollar for knocking over the milk bottles. One dollar was not enough. Even at a quarter per try, those milk bottles would not fall down. "C'mon kid, you can do it," the man kept telling me, "a little girl just did." It didn't make sense. I threw hard. I hit them well, but they wouldn't fall.

Meanwhile, Kevin was tossing darts at balloons. When he finally popped three, he pointed to the big stuffed snake that wrapped around the booth, but the lady running the game reached under the counter and gave him a plastic doll. "The snake's for five wins in a row," she said, smiling. "Ready to try again?"

Lee had stayed with me and had tried the milk bottles several times himself. "If we threw together I'll bet we could knock them off," he mumbled. The man heard him.

"I'll tell you guys what," he said, looking around carefully, "since I want you to get that teddy bear, for three dollars, you can both throw at the same time."

We had him. We knew we had him. "Deal," we said and ran to get Kevin. Three dollars was all we had between us, and as we laid it down, we laughed. Our parents would be so surprised when we did what they said could not be done.

As Lee and I took careful aim, Kevin counted. One, two, three, throw! We threw. Both balls hit squarely, but the bottles did not fall down. They rocked, they moved, they tilted, but they didn't fall. "Tough luck, guys," the man said, "try again next year."

"At least," Kevin remarked as we walked away, "we don't have to hear our dads say 'we told you so.' "

Lee stopped. "Do you really think they'd rub it in if they found out?" he asked.

"Mine would," I answered.

# Unfair Tales of Midway Madness

On Sunday morning, my father preached about the end of the world. "There will be explosions," he said, "and tornados and earthquakes. And nothing will be left standing." Then my dad looked at me and smiled. "Nothing," he continued, "but those three milk bottles at the fair."

It was in a bottle, floating near the bank
in Beauman's Pond. Reaching it with a
rake, she unscrewed the cap and read.

# A Fowl Day Ends with Thanksgiving

**E**veryone around the dinner table smiled as Pat Ward put the last dish in front of them. "I know it's not much. . . ."

The whole family laughed out loud. That statement had been made by Pat every Thanksgiving of their lives. Actually, there was enough food to feed an infantry division, but she always worried that there would be some poor soul who didn't get at least five helpings of everything.

This year, she had prepared the dressing a day earlier than usual to give her more time with the grandchildren, but she only used that time to expand the menu. Besides the turkey and dressing, Pat had baked a ham, three pumpkin pies, and a sweet potato casserole. She made fried corn, cranberry salad, squash, rolls, butter beans, and three kinds of peas.

There was a time when family members would jokingly mention a favorite dish during the days before Thanksgiving. This was

145

only a game—a challenge to see if their suggestion would end up on the table. It always did. They felt guilty about that last year when Pat cooked 6 different entrees and 11 desserts, so this year they kept quiet.

"Wade, please say grace," Pat directed as everyone bowed their heads.

"Certainly, dear. Let us pray." And as they all closed their eyes, he began. "Dear Heavenly Father, we come to you on this day of Thanksgiving with gratefulness in our hearts. . . ."

Wade paused. *This is ridiculous*, he thought. *How can I even say that? I don't feel grateful at all. I shouldn't even finish this prayer.* But he did.

Pat's husband, Wade, is more commonly known around Sawyerton Springs as Pastor Ward. He has led the flock at Beauman's Pond United Methodist Church for well over two decades now, but lately it has all been seeming a bit much. It's not that he is old—he isn't. "I'm just tired," he told Pat this morning, "and frustrated. I've had it.

"It's not necessarily the church," he tried to explain, "or Rotary Club, or my city council duties, or the grandkids. It's just, well . . . it's just everything. I've had it." Pat understood. Lately, she had kind of "had it" too.

There at the dinner table, Wade sliced the ham and looked at Pat's Uncle Frank. Uncle Frank was 74 years old and sort of a know-it-all. Uncle Frank also knew a million jokes, and as Wade finished the ham and started on the turkey, he told another one. *Another stupid joke*, Wade thought.

"So there's these cowboys," Uncle Frank was saying, "and as they rode into town whoopin' and shootin', there was this dog right in the middle of the street. One of them cowboys shot him right in the foot. A couple of days later, the cowboys was in a saloon. They was drinkin' and cussin' and playin' cards, when all of a sudden. . . ." Uncle Frank's eyes got big. "All of a sudden a shadow fell over the saloon. As the cowboys looked up, they saw the dog walking through the swinging doors. He had on a gun belt and a hat pulled down low over his eyes. A cowboy said, 'What do you want?' and the dog says 'I've come to get the man that shot my paw!' "

Everyone screamed with laughter. "I've come to get the man that shot my paw," Uncle Frank said again, banging his hand on the table. "You get it, son?" he asked Wade. "You get it, don't you? I've come to get the man that shot my paw!"

Wade forced a smile. "I get it, Uncle Frank," he said. "Would you like some turkey?"

Wade had driven all the way to Foley to pick up Uncle Frank earlier that afternoon. He had missed the first quarter of the Dallas–Detroit game because Uncle Frank insisted on leaving the house at 2:00 sharp. No reason and no way to talk him out of it. Before he even said hello, Uncle Frank had asked, "Son? If Patty Duke married Gomer Pyle, what would her name be?"

Wade shrugged.

"Patty Duke Pyle! Get it? Duke Pyle? Patty Duke Pyle!"

On the way to the house, sandwiched between the jokes, Uncle Frank had asked Wade why he was driving a 12-year-old car. "It was a piece of junk when you bought it," he said.

"It's what we can afford, Uncle Frank," Wade had answered, but inside he had been seething.

As the family ate and talked, Wade thought about the car. *Uncle Frank had been right. It was a piece of junk when he bought it. Billy Pat had told him as much when he sold it to him. "It will need repairs now and again" were Billy Pat's very words.*

*I'm 53 years old*, Wade thought. *I should not be driving a 12-year-old car. Pat is 48, and she's never had a car of her own.*

For the third year in a row, the church elders had voted down a 1,500 dollar raise in their pastor's salary. Last Monday, Roger Luker had come to tell him in person. "We just felt that the money would be of better use to foreign missions," Roger said. "After all, there are a lot of poor people overseas. And besides, it's not like you have to make a house payment—the church owns the parsonage."

Wade drifted back into the conversation on the giggles of another joke. ". . . so there was the fat lady, stuck in the window of the church. When the guy in the devil costume walked around to ask directions, she said, 'Mr. Devil, don't hurt me. I been going to this church for 40 years, but you know I been on your side all along!' "

As everyone howled, Wade thought, *There's probably some truth in there somewhere.* Through dessert, Wade wondered if his church members cared more about poor people they didn't know than they did about his family.

*That's right*, Wade said to himself, *You do own the parsonage. Where are we supposed to live when I retire? Or am I just supposed to preach 'til I'm a hundred and keel over on the pulpit? Why can't I buy my wife new dresses? Or a diamond ring? Or a new car? And about the car we're driving now—one more year and the engine will die. Then the floor will fall out, and I'll be driving around town like Fred Flintstone!*

After dinner, the family helped clean up while Wade tried to herd Uncle Frank into the car. "If I can get him out of here," Wade said to Pat, "then I'll have something to be thankful for!"

Uncle Frank's jokes were becoming a blur, and Wade easily tuned them out as he drove. The kids were on his mind. They were always after him to do something. "Daddy fix this. Daddy, can you and Mama keep the children? Daddy, we're a little short this month."

The city council thing was bugging him, too. He hadn't even wanted the position, but everyone begged him to take it. They said, "You will be a moral voice for the community, Wade, please help us!" Now they were all mad because he had voted no to having liquor at their Christmas party. What did they expect?

After Wade walked Uncle Frank to the door and listened to four more jokes, he got back in his car and drove. Had he gone

# A Fowl Day Ends with Thanksgiving

straight home, this story might have ended here (and in not too happy a fashion).

But Wade didn't go home. It wasn't until 2 a.m. the next morning that he rolled into his driveway. Pat had been frantic, but she knew her husband too well to push him for answers. She was relieved he was safe and glad to see that he was smiling. It was the first time she'd seen him really smile in days.

Wade apologized for worrying her. He said he hadn't meant to be so distant or to snap at her as he had done lately. He kissed her, looked at her, and kissed her again. Then he went to bed.

Pat might never have known what happened that night that caused such a change in Wade had she not found the letter. It was in a bottle, floating near the bank in Beauman's Pond. Pat was raking leaves behind the church when she saw it. Reaching the bottle with the rake, she unscrewed the cap, fished out the letter, and read:

*Dear God,*

*It doesn't feel like Thanksgiving. At least I don't feel very thankful. In fact, I am fairly ticked off. If you asked me "about what?"—I'd say "everything." I am so preoccupied with the things that are going wrong in my life that I am having a hard time seeing the bigger picture.*

*Lord, I'm going to sit here by this pond until you remind me of ten things I have to be thankful for. And please do it fast. Pat is going to kill me for being late.*

*1). I have Pat. She loves me even when I'm being a jerk to her relatives like I was today.*

*2). I have a home in which to live. Remind me occasionally of the people on the street.*

*3). My family has enough to eat. I know there are fathers who put their children to bed hungry.*

*4). I have people who care about me. There are many who don't.*

*5). I was born in America. With all our problems, this is still the greatest country in the world.*

6). *I can see and hear and walk and talk. These are things I rarely consider, but they are a priceless gift.*

7.) *I have the opportunity to help people who are hurting. It is amazing how much good an encouraging word can do.*

8). *I have the seasons. They are a constant reminder of change. After the winter in my life, there is always springtime.*

9). *I have my children and grandchildren who depend on me. That is an honor, and I have learned to be dependable.*

10). *I have music, trees, a good bed, a pond to fish in, my health, a car that does in fact run, clothes to wear, time with my family, and in Uncle Frank, I have an unlimited source of jokes for my sermons. Thank you, Lord, even for him.*

*—Wade*

"A new-born King to see, pa rum
pa pum pum."

# A Shining Light

For the first time in several years, snow is forecast for Sawyerton Springs. The children, as one would expect, are thrilled about the possibility of an early Christmas vacation, and even the adults, in their own way, are excited.

Miss Luna Myers has been organizing the emergency relief effort for the Grace Fellowship Baptist Church. She compiled a list of all the men who have 4-wheel drive trucks and has asked that CB channel 72 remain open for stranded townsfolk.

Rick and Sue Carper have stocked the rolling store with all kinds of non-perishables—this in addition to batteries, blankets, and candles. It is obvious that no one has forgotten the Christmas Storm of 1967.

That particular year, by the day before Christmas, most of the annual events had already taken place. The wreath competition at the garden club was won for the ninth year in a row by Martha Luker. The Yule parade, led by VFW 218, had expanded its route to seven blocks. And, of course, that was the last year that Beauman's Pond United Methodist Church presented their Singing Tree.

The Singing Tree was a huge structure—almost 50 feet tall—which allowed the Methodist choir to stand in a tree-like shape, one on top of the other. The choir perched on platforms, sticking their heads through pine limbs that had been placed there for authenticity as they sang like live decorations.

During that year's performance, with the entire town in attendance, Haywood Perkins fell from the third tier and almost broke his neck. The Singing Tree was history.

To this day, no one agrees on exactly why the tradition was dumped. The obvious answer is the danger factor, but there are a few people who still blame Miss Edna Thigpen and her editorial in the *Sawyerton Springs Sentinel*. "Is it a good idea," she asked, "to commercialize this season even in our churches? When a man with no record of clumsiness falls from a fake tree while singing 'Here Comes Santa Claus' as the minister of the congregation dances up the communion aisle dressed as the fat man himself . . . is someone trying to tell us something?" And so, after a brief discussion of church leaders, the Singing Tree was dismantled for good.

For as long as anyone can remember, the people of Sawyerton Springs have attended a Christmas Eve service at the Baptist and Methodist churches. That particular year, however, on December 23, the Baptists had somehow flooded the sanctuary at Grace Fellowship.

Pastor Wade Ward, being a friend of my dad—the Baptist minister—invited our congregation to join his Methodist flock for a combined service. "Really, Larry," Pastor Ward told my father, "it might be good for your people, you know, kind of give them a chance at a second opinion!" In any case, that is how we all came to be packed into the Methodist church that night.

The service itself was different than anything I had ever experienced. Not only was the building unfamiliar and "Holy, Holy, Holy" not the first song in the hymnal, it was the first time in my life that I had been to a church in which my father was not preaching.

Pastor Ward was a great guy. Always quick with a joke, he was one of the most popular men in town. He was then in his mid-thirties, good looking, with a touch of gray already in his hair. "Howbowcha!," he would say when he passed you on the street. "Fine, Pastor," we would answer, and he'd be on his way.

I asked my mom once why everyone called Pastor Ward "Pastor" and they called my dad "Brother. " "Isn't Dad a pastor, too?" I asked.

"Yes," Mom replied with a smile.

"And what about Pastor Ward," I continued, "I bet he has a brother."

"Right again," she said.

"Then why . . . ."

I went on like that for about ten more minutes. My mother was a very patient woman.

Altogether, the service was wonderful. We sang "O Little Town of Bethlehem" and "It Came Upon a Midnight Clear." Pastor Ward even asked my father to pray.

The evening was also a success for me personally. Though I was only eight years old at the time, I had already become addicted to making my friends laugh. That night, not only were my usual targets in attendance—Kevin Perkins, Lee Peyton, and the Luker boys—I had a new audience as well.

The Methodist kids, Wayne Gardner, Steve Krotzer, and the others, were helpless in my grasp. Weird noises during the sermon, cow sounds during "Away in a Manger," everything I did worked that night. They literally laughed out loud. From the choir, their parents gave them the "wait 'til I get you home" look as I managed my usual straight face.

The big hit of the night, in my opinion, was my version of "We Three Kings." In a voice just loud enough for my friends to hear, I sang:

*We three kings of orient are*
*Tried to smoke a loaded cigar*
*It went boom and we went zoom*
*All through the ladies bathroom.*

Wayne, Steve, and the rest of them doubled over the pews as I kept singing—looking for all the world as if I were appalled at their behavior.

As the last carol was sung, the big double doors in the back of the sanctuary were swung open. I will never forget the sight they revealed. Snow. I had never seen it before. Snow—just like on television. White, soft, and covering everything, it was, at the time, the most incredible thing I had ever seen.

No one said a word as we all stood there looking. The trees around Beauman's Pond appeared to be covered with frosting. The cars in the parking lot all looked alike, and the road was not even visible as the snow continued to fall in great swirling sheets.

Finally, from the middle of the group crowded around the door, someone broke the silence. It was Pastor Ward. "Lord," he said, "we are amazed!"

Not to be outdone, I suppose, my father also spoke. "Lord," he said, "We are in awe!"

Then we heard another voice. It was Dr. Peyton. "Lord," he said, "We are stuck!"

It was true. We were snowed in! Now, one must realize that there were only two or three inches on the ground, but to us, it might as well have been two or three feet. Snow in south Alabama is like rain in Los Angeles or grits in New York—a rare occurrence.

Once, when I was in the first grade, a teacher thought she saw a flurry. All the kids were packed up and sent home. "A snow storm is dangerous!" I was told. And now, here we were, everyone in town snowbound together in one building. At least we were in church—God save us all!

# A Shining Light

"I think I can make it," Tom Henley said. "I can get help." For a moment we stared at him. Then a voice from the back of the room asked, "Who you gonna call, Tom? We're all here."

Tom thought about that for a bit, then said, "I'm going anyway. I'm not spending Christmas here," and with that he trudged into the parking lot. At first, he couldn't find his car. As he brushed the snow from several others, Mr. Rawls yelled to him, "Be sure to clean mine, Tom!" We all laughed.

Finally, he found his Oldsmobile, got it to crank, and after bouncing off four other vehicles, Tom returned to the safety of the church. "We'll never get out of here," he said. "We're doomed."

"Well, I might have gotten through," Miss Luna said, "if you hadn't of knocked my truck into the ditch!"

"Next time don't park by the ditch," he replied.

"I wouldn't be here at all," Miss Luna fumed, "if you Methodists hadn't of opened your big mouths. Who needs your invitation? God tried to tell us to stay home!"

"Listen here," he said as he started toward her.

"Tom!" a voice rang out. It was Pastor Ward. "We'll have none of that. Everyone, please, come back in and settle down."

For a while, we all just sat there. What would people in Minnesota do in this situation, we wondered. Roger Luker began to cry. Maybe because he was scared or maybe because Kevin Perkins told him that Santa Claus would be skipping us this year. I was scared, too. Some of the adults began to argue about what to do and who got us in this mess in the first place and whether or not anybody had food we could ration. People were nervous, and they were beginning to take it out on each other.

Suddenly, everyone quieted down. Someone was singing.

"Come, they called him, pa rum pa pum pum."

Where was that coming from? We looked at each other.

"A new-born King to see, pa rum pa pum pum."

There it was again, a tiny voice, from the corner of the church.

"Our finest gifts to bring, pa rum pa pum pum."

We crept closer to the voice. It was so soft, yet it cut through our tension and irritability like a knife.

"To lay before the King, pa rum pa pum pum, rum pa pum pum, rum pa pum pum."

It was Jill Perkins, Kevin's younger sister, daughter of Haywood and Louise. In the midst of the bickering and worry, the five year old had crawled under a pew and was singing her favorite carol.

As we gathered around her, Pastor Ward urged, "Keep singing, honey." And she did.

"Come, they called him, pa rum pa pum pum."

Soon, we all joined in. Those who didn't know the words kept the beat with a steady "prrum, prrum, prrum, prrum."

It was a magical moment. People who rarely spoke to each other were smiling and holding hands. I looked at my mother— she had tears in her eyes. Over and over we sang the song until finally, it was quiet. Pastor Ward took a deep breath. "And a little child shall lead them," he said.

"Joy to the world, the Lord is come. . . ." someone sang and everyone joined in. We sang for hours that Christmas Eve, and I remember noticing after a while that it no longer seemed cold. There was a warmth in that place, that night, that will last a lifetime. It was a flame rekindled by a little girl who reminded us of how much we really love each other, how much we really care.

As I laid my head in my mother's lap and drifted off to sleep, the last thing I heard was my mom and dad singing. Their voices mingled with those of other parents who were also holding their sleeping children.

"Oh, the weather outside is frightful, but our fire is so delightful. And since we've no place to go—let it snow, let it snow, let it snow!"

"You . . . You're dying?" Sharon asked
in a soft voice. "What's wrong?"

# Dying for a Valentine's Date

I was in love. Her name was Sharon Holbert, and she was the prettiest girl I had seen in nine years. Her beautiful face, framed by short, dark hair, was covered with freckles, and the flat sandals she wore slapped the ground like firecrackers when she ran. And when she ran, Sharon was faster than any boy in our third grade class.

The first time I saw her was on the playground. At the time, she was beating Lee Peyton within an inch of his life. She seemed almost elegant—sitting there on his back punching his head. It was at that moment that I knew she would be mine. She was incredible.

Around October of that year, I asked a friend of Sharon's to ask her if she would "go" with me. I wasn't really certain what it meant to "go" with someone, but I had heard that if you "went"

161

with a person, you couldn't "go" with someone else. That sounded good to me.

During first recess, her friend popped the question. I watched them talking from across the playground. I saw my intermediary point at me as Sharon squinted, trying to get a better look. Actually, I watched this drama unfold upside down.

"You know him, Sharon," her friend seemed to be saying. "He's the one hanging by his knees on the monkey bars. You know, the cool one."

Luckily, Sharon told her friend to tell me that, yes, she would "go" with me. The bell rang and we ran back into class.

Arithmetic held no interest for me that day. Who really cared what 10 minus 3 equals? Not me, that was for sure. Sharon Holbert was all mine. She would walk with only me, be on my team for relay races, and beat up who I asked her to—she was mine.

During lunch, I winked at my woman from across the lunchroom. She turned red. *Love is wonderful*, I thought. Then, at second recess, Sharon told her friend to tell me that we were breaking up.

I was crushed. What had gone wrong? We had such a good relationship. Maybe it was a lack of communication. All I knew was that the girl of my dreams had been mine for three-and-a-half hours, and I had never spoken to her.

Sharon continued to be the object of my love for the next several years. *One day*, I thought, *she would love me, too. I would change. I would become the man of her dreams.*

Was I not handsome enough? In the fourth grade I grew sideburns—hair that grew down past my ear lobes, which I kept wet and pointed just like the crew on "Star Trek." I knew Sharon liked "Star Trek," and I went to school every day looking just like Captain Kirk.

I also tried to curl the hair on the back of my neck to look more like Bobby Sherman. I did this by putting my hands behind my head, folding my hair up, and pressing as hard as I could. This process didn't actually curl my hair so much as it made it stick straight out. Another year went by, and, unbelievably, as good as I looked, Sharon was not impressed.

Maybe, I thought in the fifth grade, I don't have the proper family background. So I told everyone that Elvis Presley was my uncle. I hadn't said anything until now, I explained, because whenever Uncle Elvis came to Sawyerton Springs, he like to keep it quiet. And besides, I told Sharon, my mother, Joyce Presley Andrews, had asked me not to tell.

Not surprisingly, none of my classmates believed me. In fact, after a few weeks of recounting my adventures with Uncle Elvis, the prevailing request seemed to be, "Prove it."

Fortunately for me, Mr. Michael Ted Williams—the town's biggest Elvis fan—had given me a picture of the King for my seventh birthday. I found it stuck between some old comic books. With a ball point pen, I wrote: "To my nephew Andy, who I have a good time doing things with—from your uncle, Elvis."

The next day, Kevin Perkins wanted desperately to believe me (even though he said Elvis wrote like a fifth grader), but the object of the exercise, Sharon, was not impressed.

During the sixth grade I wrote songs. Intending to dazzle her with creativity, I composed masterpieces like, "You've Lost That Lovin' Feeling," "Cathy's Clown," "Smoke Gets in Your Eyes," and many more. My parent's record collection was a huge source of inspiration as I put the lyrics on paper.

At this point, I felt I was gaining a little ground. Sharon seemed genuinely interested in me. I was knocking out the hits once or twice every week and passing them to Kevin during English class. He passed them to her during history.

This might have gone on indefinitely had I not seen Sharon in our church one Sunday. Her family was Methodist, but there was Sharon—sitting with her friend Glenda Johnson in the third row, surrounded by Baptists. I thought she might be trying to get a double dose. The next day, wanting to show her how religious I was, I gave her a new song I had just written. It was to tuck in her Bible, I suggested.

With the hindsight of three decades giving me much clearer vision, I doubt if I would have chosen the same song to "write" for Sharon's Bible. She, of course, recognized the words, realized that she had been suckered, and was not impressed. I wonder if a sixth grader today could get away with claiming copyright to "Onward Christian Soldiers."

For a long time, Sharon didn't speak to me. I suffered a severe case of writer's block and never wrote another song. Elvis also stopped dropping by about that time. But I still had my side-burns, if not my beloved.

The summer of our sixth grade year came and went. Sharon had spent her vacation at camp, so I hadn't seen her for three months. When she returned, she was more beautiful than ever. She was also about a foot-and-a-half taller.

While we had been relatively the same height in May, all of a sudden, in September, I was saying, "Hi, Sharon," to her collar-bone. She was a giant. Or I was a midget—I wasn't sure which.

Seventh grade was tough enough without this humiliation. It got even worse when Wayne Gardner asked her to "go" with him and she said yes. He asked her himself! He walked right up to Sharon (I was standing there) and over my head said, "Hey. You wanna go with me?"

"I guess," she said.

He said, "Groovy," and walked off.

That Wayne was something else. I was intimidated. For one thing, he was as tall as Sharon, and for another, he was in the eighth grade. He was worldly. He played football. He had been around.

The Wayne-Sharon match-up lasted until the first of December. Wayne told everyone he broke up so he wouldn't have to buy her a Christmas present. That made me mad, and I told him so. He

# Dying for a Valentine's Date

pushed me in a ditch and laughed.

As February rolled around, I eyed the 14th with optimism. That was the day that Grace Fellowship Baptist Church held the annual Valentine's banquet, and as a seventh grader, I was now eligible to attend.

In the hall one afternoon, by her locker, I asked Sharon to be my date. "To what?" she asked.

"To the Grace Fellowship Baptist Church Annual Valentine's Banquet," I answered. "What do you say?"

"Well . . ." She hesitated.

I was not going without a date, and this was the only date I wanted. I stepped up the attack: "C'mon, please? We'll have a great time. And besides, I'm dying . . ." I paused to catch my breath, and in that moment I saw Sharon's eyes open wide.

Now, understand, after my breath, I was intending to complete my thought, which was something like, "I'm dying to see the Great Gossamer, who is a Christian magician we are having at the banquet." That was my intention.

But as I watched Sharon's eyes fly open and her face go pale, I knew immediately what had happened. I took advantage of it.

"You . . . You're dying?" Sharon asked in a soft voice.

Looking down at my feet and then up into her incredible tear-filled eyes, I said, "Yes. Yes, I am."

"What's wrong?" she asked.

And in an answer that wasn't exactly a lie, I said, "It's my heart."

The night of the 14th, I walked up the sidewalk in front of Sharon's house. I wore black-and-white plaid pants with a red shirt. the cream-colored sport coat matched the hearts on my black-and-cream tie. My belt was white. It complemented my shoes, which were white with gold buckles on the side. I looked good.

I carried a corsage. My mother, who waited in the car, had coached me on giving it to my date and what to do after the corsage had been presented. At the door, I was perfect.

165

"Sharon," I gushed, "You are more beautiful than the flowers I brought."

Then I addressed Sharon's mother. "Mrs. Holbert," I said, "Will you pin this on her dress? I am so clumsy sometimes. By the way, what time would you like me to have her home?"

Sharon's mother rubbed her mouth with her hand to hide her smile. "About 9:30 would be fine," she said.

The banquet was memorable. The chicken was broiled, which was not really the way I liked it, but as Sharon pointed out, it was better for my heart. The Great Gossamer truly was great. He made an analogy between sawing a woman in half and the magic of the Lord in our lives.

When it was all over, my mother drove us to get ice cream and then on to Sharon's house. As I walked her to the door, Sharon said, "You aren't really dying are you?"

"Yes," I answered. "I mean no. No, I'm not. Not soon anyway."

She smiled. "My mother told me that you weren't. She said you were just trying to get me to like you."

As we reached the door, I was silent. Sharon continued. "You don't have to say that stuff to get me to like you, you know. I always kinda have anyway. Thanks for tonight." And with that, she kissed me and ran inside. I stood there for a few minutes not believing what I had just experienced. She liked me. She said so right before she kissed me. And it wasn't an ordinary kiss either. It was right near the mouth.

I walked back to the car that night a different young man. I carried with me a confidence that can only be given by a girl. Through the years, Sharon remained my friend even though we never "went" with each other or anything close to that. But I'll always remember that Valentine's Day, and I'll always remember what I told my mother as I crawled into the front seat. I shut the door behind me, grinned, and said, "She was impressed."

*At first, people were suspicious—it had been a long time since anyone had handed out $5 bills on Main Street.*

# On the Bandwagon

There has been a flurry of activity in town this past month. According to the *Sawyerton Springs Sentinel*—"The State's Eighth Oldest Newspaper"—the descendants of Frank and Jo Marie Planke got together recently for a family reunion. It was held in the fellowship hall of Beauman's Pond United Methodist Church. All the Plankes under 70 years of age brought a covered dish. This was page one news.

On page two, there was a mention of Katrina Anderson's recent bout with allergies and a detailed account of Granger Clark's heart attack, under the headline GRANGER IN BAD SHAPE. The article went on to give Dr. Peyton's assessment of the situation, which was "stable," but it also included Miss Luna's opinion that "things don't look good for Granger."

Page three included a list of people whose subscriptions to the *Sentinel* had expired. There were 23 of them—their names and addresses in bold print. Everyone knows that their name will stay in the paper until they renew, so they usually pay up quickly.

The one exception is Roger Luker. He and his wife, Carol, have been on the list for almost nine years. He told Billy Pat Williams that he never read the *Sentinel* anyway and wasn't about to pay a "fine" to Miss Edna just to get his name out of the paper like everyone else did. "So that is that," Billy Pat remembers him saying. And after nine years, most people in town believe he meant it.

The classified section, also on page three, offered babysitting by Janelle Williams, Billy Pat's daughter, and a flashing arrow sign for rent by Tom Henley. Daphne Deas is selling a full set of Mossy Oak camouflage (boots included) that Jeff gave her for Christmas, and someone is looking to buy a good bird dog. Whoever it is, however, did not include a name or number in the ad.

At the bottom of the page, as always, was the advertisement to stuff envelopes in your own home and make up to $2,000 per week. And directly under that advertisement, as always, was the note from Miss Edna Thigpen asking us to ignore the ad.

"Warning!" it says. "This offer comes from somebody in Chicago and is probably a rip-off. They do, however, pay $100 for the space and have never been late with their money. As long as that continues, we will run this ad, but as responsible members of our community, we feel the need to inform you, our public, that they are more than likely crooks. Signed, The Editor."

In addition to the usual talk, most of the excitement around town this month has been centered on the *Sentinel's* back page (page four), where the announcement about the band fundraiser was printed. For the past three years, the Sawyerton Springs High School Barracuda Marching Band has been raising money for new uniforms. Now only $650 shy of their goal, most people believe this will be the last year the kids will have to appear in borrowed outfits. "Won't it be great," Ginny Williams said to the Band Mothers Committee, "to see all 23 of our kids in uniforms the right size and color?"

The Band Mothers Committee consists of Ginny, Sandy Pratt,

# On the Bandwagon

Daphne Deas, and Liz Reed. Only Ginny actually has a teenager in the band, but Sandy and Daphne have younger children who will one day benefit from the program, and Liz is Max Reed's wife.

Max, the owner of Max's Mortuary, is also the band director. Several years ago when the principal, George Keep, found out that Max had attended college on a tuba scholarship, he asked him to form a band for the school. "C'mon, Max," George pleaded, "at our home football games, a lot of people are leaving during halftime. We've got to have something to keep them there!" So Max agreed to help.

When he began, there were no uniforms at all. For a year, Max had the kids wear blue jeans and white T-shirts with a pack of cigarettes rolled up in their sleeves. They played fifties music so it would appear the clothes had been planned. During the third quarter of the last game of the season, Brad Rollins, the trumpet player, actually lit one of the cigarettes and smoked it. After that, Max assured the principal that he'd come up with something else.

And he did. The band wore their parent's old military uniforms and played patriotic songs. The following season, it was cowboy hats and country music. The year after that, it was bathing suits and the hits of the Beach Boys. Since most of the band stayed sick that year, the decision was made to use the old uniforms of nearby Foley High.

The uniforms were not in the best of shape, and the kids hated wearing the colors of a rival school, but, as Max explained, "It's either blue and gold or pneumonia—take your pick." In any case, those are the uniforms still being worn by the Barracuda Marchers.

"So, what do we do this year?" Ginny asked as she opened the meeting. "We sold chocolate bars and candles last year. Before that it was Christmas trees and brass-plated social security cards."

Liz sipped her coffee and mused, "We've had car washes, spaghetti suppers, and Halloween carnivals. I like my social security card. Do you think that company could do church bulletins in brass? They would make great mementos."

"We could sell old clothes," Daphne suggested.

Sandy laughed. "Daphne, most of the people in town are already wearing old clothes. I know I don't want any more!"

"How about a raffle?" Sandy asked.

"Nothing to raffle," Daphne answered.

"Well, we'd better come up with something," Liz said, "or just divide the money up and give it back to everybody."

For a moment, the ladies were silent. Then Ginny's eyes widened. "That's a great idea!"

"What?" they all asked. "What is a great idea?"

"Remember that story in the Bible," Ginny said, "where the guy gave three other guys the talents?"

"Talents are like dollars, right?" Liz asked.

"Right," Ginny said. "Anyway, he told them to take the talents and multiply them, and he rewarded the guy who increased profits the most."

"Now how does that relate to us?" Sandy asked.

"Don't you see? We can take the money we've already made, give everybody in town five dollars, and see what they can do."

"It might work," Daphne said, looking at Sandy.

Ginny stood up. "It *will* work. Liz, withdraw all the money from the bank. Get it in fives. We'll stay here and make a list of people to involve. Hurry back!"

At first, people were suspicious—it had been a long time since anyone had handed out $5 bills on Main Street. But, after an explanation from the band mothers, and particularly after the *Sentinel* came out, they all calmed down. Unfortunately, most of them also took a "wait-and-see" attitude.

The people who did choose to participate were told that they had 30 days to do something with their money. "This is an investment in yourself and in our children," read the copy in the paper. They were enthusiastic, but there was a very vocal group who disagreed with the concept altogether. They felt that this type of

# On the Bandwagon

thing was the board of education's responsibility. And besides, they said, it'll never work.

"Who cares what they think," Billy Pat told Ginny over lunch. "Anytime we try to accomplish something good, the critics come out of the woodwork. They are real good at telling us what's wrong with something, but they don't ever *do* anything. It's like a guy who knows the way, but can't drive the car. This idea will work if we do!"

There turned out to be only 17 people who actually participated in the project, and for a time, Ginny was depressed. But she soon saw the incredible results that can be achieved by a few people with a common goal.

Kathy Rollins took her money and bought flour and yeast. She made loaves of homemade bread and sold them all over town. When she sold all the bread, she took a little of the money, bought more flour and yeast, and repeated the process. At the end of the month, Kathy turned in $38. Glenda Perkins bought a white flower pot, painted a sunset on it, and sold it for $10. She did the same thing four more times and made $40.

Bubba Pratt took $5 worth of wood and made two walking canes. Sandy painted them, and by turning the money over several times during the month, they made $62. Sandy also took in an additional $27 doing needlepoint.

Tom Henley sold soft drinks in his hardware store. He made $31.50. Norman Green bought cat litter and cleaned oil from driveways at $4 a pop. He made $84. Billy Pat took a can of car wax and turned it into $160. Several of his friends said it was worth 20 bucks to watch Billy Pat work on their cars. It was worth it to Billy Pat, too.

In fact, it was worth it to everyone. Sue Carper was so proud she was able to hand Ginny $49 that she had tears rolling down her face. "I know I don't have a child in the band," she said, "But thank you for letting me be a part of something this worthwhile."

As everyone turned in their money last Friday night, the 17

173

people who stuck it out and made their idea work were awed by what they had accomplished. As they laid the bills and change out on a small card table in the band room, they clapped and cheered.

Kevin Perkins: carved wooden dominoes, $50.

Jeff Deas: selling tomato plants, $39.

Liz Reed: prune cakes, $44.

Max Reed: homemade peanut brittle, $28.

George Keep: shining shoes, $53.

Marian Keep: manicures, $24.

Wade Ward: refinishing furniture, $61.

Jerry Anderson: painting deck rails, $40.

Rebecca Peyton: ceramics, $33.

The Super 17, as they had been calling themselves, raised $814.50, which was certainly enough to cover the band uniforms for their children. But as I see it, they did something far more important. Long after the new uniforms are tattered and faded, the children of Sawyerton Springs will remember the example of 17 adults who found a way to make things work.

The critics turned their backs, the skeptics laughed, but the uniforms are bought and paid for. Never underestimate the power of a group of people who have a dream fueled by enthusiasm. Bubba had it right when he told Miss Luna in an exclusive interview for the *Sentinel*, "Whether we think we can or we think we can't . . . either way we're right!"

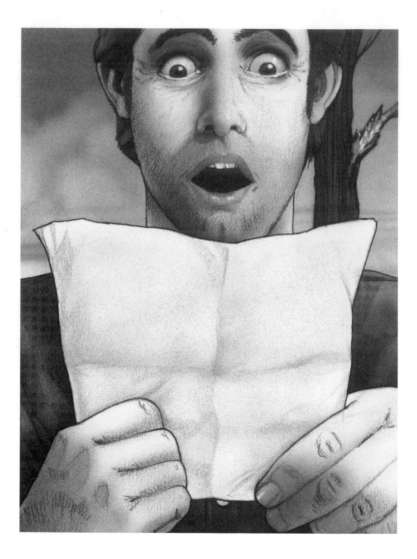

*"Good gosh-a-mighty! If that deed weren't so old, Kevin Perkins would own this town!"*

# The Treasure of the Oak

When lightning hit the big oak tree behind Norman's Groceteria, everyone in town woke up. No one immediately knew what had been struck, but there was no question that something had taken a direct blow.

As Bubba Pratt jumped out of bed, his first thought was that Cabell Outlaw had finally blown up his gas station. Bubba has warned Cabell for 20 years about smoking near the pumps. Shaking the cobwebs from his head, however, he quickly realized that what he heard had been closer than Cabell's station.

Liz Reed screamed in her sleep when the lightning struck. The combination of the boom and her reaction to it propelled her husband, Max, toward the ceiling. When he hit the floor, he was in his pants. They were on backwards, but they were on. Frozen in a karate stance, Max was ready to fight. Exactly who, he was not yet awake enough to decide.

Jeff Deas was parked in front of Henley's Hardware when the storm came up. As the lightning and thunder grew worse, he drove his patrol car toward home. Passing Norman's on the left, he saw the flash in his rearview mirror and thought the store had been hit, but as he wheeled around for a better look, he saw that the groceteria was fine. The tree, on the other hand, was split right down the middle.

Straining to see through the rain, Jeff directed his headlights toward the old tree. From what he could tell, there was no fire to take care of—it was raining too hard for that—but, come morning, there would be a lot of cleaning up to do.

Jeff parked and waited under the overhang at Norman's for the rest of the guys he knew would soon arrive. In a town like Sawyerton Springs, all the emergency services operate on a volunteer basis. There is a volunteer fire department, a volunteer ambulance crew, and, of course, Jeff is the volunteer policeman. *As loud as that was,* Jeff thought, *everybody will be here.*

He was right. It didn't take long for Bubba and Max to show up. They were joined by Billy Pat Williams, Dr. Lee Peyton, Kevin Perkins, and Norman, who opened the store and made coffee for everybody.

"I built a tree house in that tree when I was in the fourth grade," Lee said as he poured coffee for Kevin. "This is kinda sad."

"My granddaddy built a tree house in it, too," Bubba said.

Kevin tore open a packet of sugar. "That oak and the General's Oak over by Beauman's Pond are supposed to be the oldest trees in this part of the state. More than 400 years old, they say."

"Who's they?" Norman asked.

"Oh, you know," Kevin replied, "they . . . everybody . . . seriously, this tree is over 400 years old."

"Well, it's been here as long as the town has, that's for sure," Billy Pat said. "Ginny has a drawing my great uncle gave her of Main Street and College Avenue in 1852. The tree's on it plain as day. And it was big then."

"Four hundred years old," Max said, shaking his head. "Well, we'll be cutting it up for firewood tomorrow. See you guys about 8:00?" They nodded, and after talking a while longer, drifted back home.

The next morning, the lack of darkness and rain made it easier to see what had happened, but it was no less tragic. The lightning bolt had taken the old tree right in the main crotch and literally split the trunk in two. One half remained upright as if nothing had touched it.

"Is there any way to save this part that's standing?" Bubba asked Kevin as they walked around the tree.

Kevin shook his head no. "Too much trauma to the whole system," he answered.

Kevin was about to pull the cord on the chain saw when Jeff yelled, "Hey, you guys! Come look at this!" He was pointing to a place in the main trunk about 15 feet above his head. As they gathered around to look, Jeff said, "It looks like glass."

Protruding about three inches from the white, shiny wood that had once been the middle of the tree was the rounded edge of . . . something…and it did in fact appear to be glass. Upon closer inspection with a ladder, the object was determined to be just that. It was a greenish-colored jar and there was something in it.

Examination of the tree explained how the jar became entombed in the first place. Someone, years ago, had evidently placed the jar into a hollow in the tree and neglected to retrieve it. As the years passed, the tree simply grew around the jar and only the lightning of the night before revealed its secret.

The rest of the morning was spent carefully sawing and hacking the wood away from the jar. It was lunch time when Billy Pat finally separated wood and glass and held up the jar. The 30 or so people who had gathered to watch cheered. "Should we open it now?" he asked.

"Yes, do it!" they urged. Throughout the morning, among the

gathering crowd, speculation as to what the jar contained had reached a fever pitch. The consensus of the group was "treasure." Exactly what kind of treasure was a source of disagreement.

Sue Carper thought it might be Native American gold, but Jerry Anderson, who is Choctaw, assured her that if his ancestors ever had gold in the first place, they wouldn't have stuck it in a tree.

Several people agreed with Pastor Ward's theory that it was probably money from a bank robbery. However, no one was able to remember any bank that had been robbed.

Moonshine, gold, fishing worms, and a murder weapon were all discussed as possibilities, but when the lid was pried off the jar, there were only three pieces of paper inside.

The first piece was a picture of Mack and Edna Sawyer, the original couple to settle near the springs in 1838. The picture was dated 1864. Also in the picture were their daughters Joyce and Barbara and their son Thomas.

The second piece of paper was a plat of the town. As Billy Pat carefully unfolded it, he saw areas that were shaded and marked "Sawyer." The largest shaded area was the part of town in which most of the present businesses were located.

The final document to be extracted from the jar was a deed. The deed gave ownership of the shaded areas on the plat to any male directly descended from the union of Mack and Edna Sawyer. Any Sawyer land, according to the document, was to be surrendered upon demand. Furthermore, the deed provided for unauthorized sale of the property by demanding lease payments of $100 per year for interim use. It was signed by Mack Sawyer and notarized by Jefferson Davis, president of the Confederate States of America.

As they all pushed in to see the amazing contents of the jar, Jeff said, "Good gosh-a-mighty! If that deed weren't so old, Kevin Perkins would own this town!" Everyone laughed. It was common knowledge that Kevin was the only living descendant of the founders.

"Yeah, that'd be a pretty good deal," Kevin said, chuckling. "I've always wanted to own my own town."

Suddenly, Max spoke up. He peered over his glasses and said, "Actually, Kev, I think you do."

While everyone had been joking about the deed and its implications, Max had been reading the fine print. Max looked at the crowd, noted their open mouths, and continued. "Knowing what I do about the law, and having studied Confederate land holdings in college, there is little doubt what has happened here. Mr. Sawyer had this particular deed signed by his president toward the end of the Civil War. If you know anything at all about history, you know that deeds of this type were upheld by federal courts when the Union was preserved."

"So what does that mean to us, Max?" Bubba asked.

"Well," Max said slowly, "It means that just about every business in this town owes Kevin around $130,000 for use of property, which, by the way, is still his."

They blinked, then looked at Kevin, who said, "I don't take Mastercard, and I don't take American Express."

All that afternoon, the town was in an uproar. The deed was the only topic of discussion. Kevin, as the president of Perkins Construction, had built almost every home in Sawyerton Springs— now he apparently owned them all as well. Everyone had an opinion about the situation.

Lee Peyton said that he was inclined to ignore it, but Bubba pointed out that Lee's home was not among those in question. "Easy for you to ignore it," he said.

Jeff offered to arrest Kevin on some trumped-up charge and "just get him the heck out of town." But no, they decided, there was Glenda and the children to think about.

Miss Luna Myers told everybody she saw that this was "of the Lord." "His hand," she said, "chopped that tree in half to reveal His will to us."

"I suppose you could see it that way," Pastor Ward remarked. "I just hope the Lord realizes that he gave Kevin His house, too!"

Meanwhile, Kevin had not indicated whether he intended to hold anyone to the terms of his newly found windfall. In fact, he had not been around town all afternoon. Being a contractor, he was busy inspecting Peg Harvey's lightning-damaged home outside of town.

Peg was a widow with three children, and now her home, which was barely adequate to begin with, had a hole in its roof. "I can pay you a little at a time, Mr. Perkins," Peg told Kevin as he surveyed the damage. "I have several sewing jobs coming up."

"We'll get it done tomorrow, Peg, and don't you worry about where the money is coming from. I don't think this'll cost anything." Kevin left her standing there with tears running down her face. As he cranked up his truck, he hoped someone would be of a mind to help Glenda if one day something happened to him.

By the next evening, Peg's roof was fixed, and there was a new oven and freezer inside the house. The freezer was filled to the top with food. Peg's children were wearing new clothes, and each had a new winter coat. Peg had enough sewing jobs to last a year, as well as extra material for several dresses of her own.

Back in town, the people of Sawyerton Springs went to bed that night having bought their property back from Kevin for $35 each. When he had explained the purpose of the transaction, many townsfolk argued that their land and homes were worth more and insisted on making up the difference. There was even enough left to start a college fund for Peg's kids.

"What a great place to live," Kevin said to Glenda as he turned out the light. And as he swung the covers over both of them, he added, "Even if I don't own it anymore."

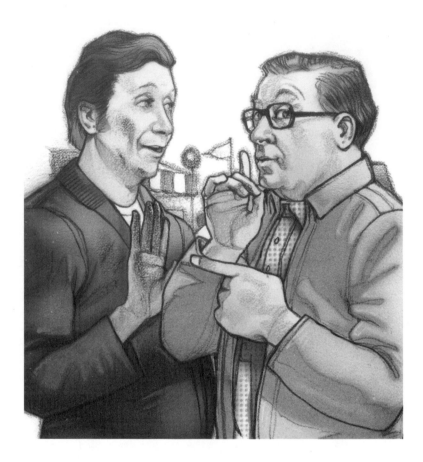

"You know, Max," he said, "I'm embarrassed to say this, but I always thought of you guys in the South as kind of dull or slow, but you're not."

# Off the Road Again

Howard and Sonya Peel exited the interstate and immediately heard a thump under the hood of their Mercedes. They looked at each other. Howard shrugged and continued talking. "Anyway, we're almost there, so we might as well get off the main road and see a little bit of the country." They heard another thump.

Sonya glanced sideways at her husband. "Is something wrong with the car?" she asked. "Maybe we should go back to that service station at the exit."

"Nah," Howard answered. "We're fine. It's probably just bad gas. It'll work itself out."

Thirty minutes later, Sonya said, "Nah, we're fine. It's probably just bad gas. It'll work itself out." They were walking at the time.

The Peels are from Chicago. Howard worked as an account executive for a Fortune 500 company while Sonya had raised the kids. They were both in their fifties now, and their children were grown.

For the last twenty or so years, Howard and Sonya have taken their family to the Gulf coast for two weeks every Memorial Day. This, however, was the first time they had gone alone.

Howard wanted it to be a special trip. He felt that Sonya deserved some spontaneity in her life. He had certainly provided her with luxuries. She drove a Mercedes and shopped at the finest stores in Chicago, but he wanted her to see a different side of the world. That's why he had decided to get off the interstate.

"Would you mind telling me why you got off the interstate?" Sonya asked as she hobbled down the road in high heels. "I mean, here we are, in the middle of southeast nowhere—walking into God only knows what kind of situation. Do you realize that something has happened on every trip we have taken in the last twenty years? At least we're not lost. Most of the time we're lost, and it's always because you won't ask for directions."

As Sonya babbled on, venting her anger, Howard thought about what she was saying. *She's right*, he mused. *At least about me not asking directions. Why won't I do that?* He suspected it was a "man" thing. He couldn't ever remember asking for directions.

Howard tuned her back in. *What was she saying?* he thought. *Oh, the bathroom deal again.* Sonya was now talking about how Howard had not stopped at a rest area an hour ago. She had needed to go then, and now she was mad about it. Howard guessed that that was another "man" thing. He would never stop if he had a choice. It was a waste of time. He had a schedule.

"Here comes a car," Howard said, looking over his shoulder.

"Well, don't stare at them, they might stop," Sonya said, suddenly frightened.

"You'd rather keep walking?" Howard raised his eyebrows.

They turned and faced the car, which was obviously intending to stop anyway. It pulled onto the grass as Max Reed rolled down the window. "You folks need a lift, I bet," Max said. "I saw your car a couple of miles back. Hop in."

"Where are you headed?" Howard asked. He was not about to trust just anyone. He was from the city—he had better sense

# Off the Road Again

than that.

"I'm going home," Max answered. "Be more than happy to give you a ride into town. By the way, my name is Max Reed."

"What is the next town?" Sonya asked.

Max was getting a little impatient. He knew from their accent that they were not from Foley or anywhere close, but they sure did seem distrustful. "Sawyerton Springs, ma'am. It's only six and a half miles up the road. 'Course, if you'd rather walk . . . ."

"No, no," they said and scrambled into the car. Sonya sat in the front, Howard in the back. He wanted to keep an eye on Max. *He seems like a nice enough guy,* Howard thought, *but you never know—he might have a body in the trunk.*

"So, Max, what do you do for a living?" Howard asked.

"I'm a mortician," Max said, and he hit the gas.

Entering town, Sonya had noticed the welcome sign: SAWYERTON SPRINGS . . . A TOWN YOU WILL LIKE. Sonya wasn't so sure. Max had already told them that they were stuck at least until tomorrow morning, but Howard refused to accept it. He insisted that they stop at a service station, so Max pulled into Cabell Outlaw's place—it was the only one in town.

"Hey, Cabell," Max said as they drove up, "I'm surprised you're here."

"I ain't," Cabell said, smiling. "I just ran by to get my pistol. I'm the starter for the kids' races today."

Max turned to the Peels. "The town has a Memorial Day picnic every year," he explained. "It's out by Beauman's Pond. We do sack races and stuff."

Howard nodded, then spoke to Cabell. "Mr. uh . . . Outlaw is it? I'm Howard Peel from Chicago. This is my wife, Sonya. We are on our way to the coast. Our car has broken down out on County Road 10, and we really need to get it worked on."

"Love to help you," Cabell said, "sure would, but I've got to be at the picnic in 20 minutes."

Howard bit his lip. "Is there anyone else here in town who can fix the car?"

"Yeah," Cabell answered. "Bubba Pratt could do it in a heartbeat. Jeff Deas—he's the cop—he could do it. Kevin Perkins, Rick Carper, Tom Henley . . . all them guys know cars. Miss Luna Myers could probably handle the job. She works on her own, you know."

"Great," Howard said to Max. "Let's find one of those people."

"Well, I know where to find 'em," Max said, "but it won't do you any good."

"Why is that?" Howard demanded.

"They're at the picnic," Max said as if it were something Howard should have figured out for himself. "Look, we have a nice hotel about two blocks away. Why don't I run you over there, let you check in and get freshened up, and you two can join us at the picnic. If this was an emergency, it'd be different."

Howard's face was blood red. "This is an emergency," he yelled.

"Is anybody dyin'?" Cabell asked.

"No," Howard said.

"Then it ain't no emergency," Cabell replied. "I'll see you at the picnic."

The Vine and Olive Hotel, on Main Street, is really just a big old house, but Bill and Misty Hamlett had turned it into a ten-room hotel back in 1964. It was a two-story wooden structure painted white, and it had green shutters. The huge wrap-around porch was lined with rocking chairs.

Misty said, "We won't be serving supper tonight. Everybody's eating at the picnic, but don't worry, there'll be plenty for you. Breakfast tomorrow morning at 7:30 sharp. Here's your key—Room 2. That'll be $24 in advance."

As they entered the room, Howard was relieved to see the room did have its own bathroom. *If it hadn't*, he thought, *I wouldn't turn my back on Sonya.*

# Off the Road Again

"So what do we do now?" he asked.

"The first thing I'm doing is taking off these shoes," Sonya said. "My feet are killing me. Did you notice there's no television?"

"But there is a bathroom," Howard pointed out.

There was a knock on the door. It was Bill. "Do ya'll want to ride over to the picnic with us?" he asked. "We have a horse and buggy we hook up for things like this. Come on, you'll love it. There's nothing to do here."

Seeing Bill's point immediately, Howard and Sonya decided to take him up on the offer. It was the first time either of them had ever ridden in a buggy, and to Sonya's surprise, she actually enjoyed it. "What's your horse's name?" she asked Bill.

"Governor," he said. "We named him that because of the resemblance between the part of the horse you are watching now and the face of the guy holding the office." They all laughed.

Sonya found herself enjoying Misty's company. At the picnic, Misty introduced her to several of the ladies, including Sandy Pratt, who Sonya said looked familiar. After only a few minutes of talking, they realized that Joyce Mercon, a friend of Sonya's in Chicago, had a picture of Sandy in her living room. Sandy and Joyce had grown up together.

Howard helped Bill with the buggy rides. While Bill made trips around the pond, Howard talked with the other men and watched the children play. "I've never been to a place like this," Howard said to Max. "How long have you lived here?"

"All my life," Max answered.

"Do you ever want to leave?"

"Sometimes, but only for a week or two. Our friends are here, the school is good, and the air is clean. And people look out for each other."

Howard turned and looked to where Sonya was sitting on a quilt with Misty. She was howling with laughter. He hadn't seen her that happy in a long time.

"You know, Max," he said, "I'm embarrassed to say this, but I always thought of you guys in the South as kind of dull or slow, but you're not."

"No," Max said, grinning, "and ya'll up North probably aren't all jerks either."

Just then, Cabell walked up. "Hey, Howard, hey, Max," he greeted the men. "Howard, I got through with the last race and went and towed your car in. I already got it fixed. Wadn't nothing but a hose to the fuel pump. You're ready to go, Bud!"

Howard frowned. "Cabell, I want you to do me a favor. I've never been here, but for some reason, I feel like I'm where I belong, at least for now anyway. All of a sudden, I don't want to go to the beach. I'll pay you fifty dollars not to tell my wife that the car is fixed."

Cabell smiled. "Well, I ain't charging you for the repairs," he said. "I felt bad about keeping you around here longer than you wanted in the first place. But as for telling your wife about the car, I'm sorry, but I already did."

Howard's face fell.

"But if your intention is to stick around," Cabell continued, "I don't think you have a problem. Your wife tried to give me a hundred not to tell you!"

"Well," he demanded, "you gonna throw it or not?"

# You Reap What You Throw

The tomato was in my hand. I stared at the gleaming, white front porch of the Vine and Olive Hotel. There was no one stirring in the small, ten-room hotel. It was well after midnight, but the light over the front door reached almost to the shadows where I lurked with Brian, my older and much wiser cousin. Brian held an egg.

"Well," he demanded, "you gonna throw it or not?"

Actually, I wasn't sure. I was usually a good kid. I went to church, made almost all *B*s in school, and didn't cuss much except for words like *dang* and *durn*. I visited my Aunt Ruth in the nursing home every Thursday afternoon with my mother, and I even let her kiss me on the cheek. Aunt Ruth usually had a brown dribble of snuff juice rolling down her chin.

I was a good kid. Yet, here I was, running the streets at night with an overripe Better Boy sizing up the freshly painted porch of one of my father's best friends.

*What am I doing?* I thought. Mr. and Mrs. Hamlett, the owners of the Vine and Olive, had that very afternoon brought a plate of brownies by our house. My arms slumped to my side. I just couldn't go through with it.

"No guts. No glory," Brian said, smirking.

I threw it. The tomato landed with a "whump" against the front door and splattered a large area of the still-sticky paint on the porch. Almost immediately, a light came on in an upstairs window. Brian, naturally, never threw the egg.

As we ran down the alley beside Henley's Hardware, I was confused. I had not wanted to slip out of my bedroom window an hour earlier. I had not wanted to steal a tomato from the Carper's garden, and I had not wanted to throw the tomato at the Vine and Olive. In fact, I had decided not to . . . but I had.

It must've been the "no guts, no glory" comment. Even though I was not certain what glory awaited a vegetable-throwing 11 year old, the statement had offered the opportunity to prove I had guts. *I have guts*, I said to myself. *No brains, maybe, but I do have guts.*

Brian was 12. Every summer, he spent a few days with my family in Sawyerton Springs. His mom, my mother's sister, would put him on a bus from Birmingham with a day's supply of Cheetos, 10 or 12 comic books, and a big sign around his neck that said: BRIAN.

Brian was the smartest kid I knew, and I really looked forward to his visits. He didn't have the kind of smarts that adults admired, like smart in school or smart in knowing the books of the Bible, Brian just had ideas that would've never occurred to me.

One year, Brian had shown Kevin Perkins and me how to smoke. He took us to a field behind the high school that was a virtual grove of rabbit tobacco. Per Brian's instructions, we made six crude, yet functional, rabbit tobacco cigars. Per Brian's example, I threw up after we smoked them.

The next year (I think I was 8), Brian told me that rabbit tobacco was for kids. What we needed, he explained, were real cigars. Real cigars, he said, like he smoked in Birmingham.

"What kind of cigars did Granddaddy say he wanted?" I asked Brian innocently. We were perusing the tobacco rack in Rick's Rolling Store. Brian had invented an elaborate scheme designed to fool Rick into selling us cigars. Since we were minors, I wasn't very confident in the plan, but it worked.

Brian answered, "Granddaddy said he wanted a pack of cherry-flavored Tiperillos and some apple-flavored White Owls."

We then made our selection and handed them to Rick. "These are for Granddaddy," I said. "We aren't going to smoke them." Then I paid him with 2 nickels, 1 dime, and 122 pennies.

Years later, Rick asked if I remembered buying the cigars that day. He wondered if we'd gotten sick. "I just figured that turning green was prob'ly worse punishment than what your daddy'd a done if I'd a told him," he said.

Rick was right. We did get violently ill, and in that respect, I still do not see a great difference between real cigars and rabbit tobacco rolled in a paper sack.

The next summer, Brian had an idea that was actually enjoyed by many of the people in town. The animals, however, were not amused. We captured and released every pet we could safely grab, but not before changing their appearances.

Brian put my sister's doll dresses on several of Mr. Michael Ted's cats. We caught Miss Luna Myers' white poodles and dyed them green. (Food coloring, by the way, does not wash out of dog hair.) Brian, with a black magic marker, connected the dots on the Peyton's Dalmatian while I gave their horse a gold tail with spray paint.

For a time, there were a lot of strange-looking animals walking the streets. No one really got upset either, except for Mrs. Perkins, and I can't say as how I blame her. Champ, her collie, was our masterpiece.

We borrowed my father's barber clippers and totally shaved the big dog. We did leave one strip of hair about two inches wide down the length of his back. Then we dyed it pink. Champ was a punk collie with a mohawk!

I got in quite a bit of trouble for that one. Mrs. Perkins called my dad and complained. I still think he was more aggravated about the dog hair in his clippers than he was about the actual dog, but the end result was the same—I got a whipping. Brian, meanwhile, was safely back in Birmingham.

The year I turned ten, Dad threatened to straighten me out with his belt before Brian arrived. He'd say, "That kid needs a little rawhide on the backside." Brian came anyway.

That summer we held our own carnival. We set it up in our backyard and charged a dime for any kid who wanted to come. The games all cost a nickel. We had ring tosses, bean-bag throws, and a candy bar walk—which is just like a cake walk except that you use candy bars. We even had a BB gun range with one of my sister's teddy bears as the target and prize. I was nervous about that, but Brian bent the sights on the gun so that no one would win. No one did.

We made almost ten dollars at the carnival. Brian took about eight of that because, he explained, it was his idea. I didn't really mind though. It was a lot of fun right up until Steve Luker figured out that the BB gun was rigged and hit me in the stomach. My dad said I deserved it.

Considering the amount of trouble my cousin had gotten me into over the years, it's still hard to understand why I continued to listen to him. But I did. His powers of persuasion were of legendary proportions. Brian could take the most idiotic concept, and after 15 minutes of his logic, I would think, *That sounds like a great idea!*

That particular gift of Brian's was why I now found myself running toward home in the middle of the night. "Do you think he saw us?" I said, wheezing.

"Who?" Brian asked.

"Mr. Hamlett," I snapped. "Who do you think I'm talking about? Do you think he saw us?"

"Nah. No way," Brian answered.

When we arrived home, we climbed through the window and into my bedroom. It was pitch dark inside the room, but we quickly got into bed. For a few minutes we just laid there. Then, I spoke. "You reckon we'll get caught?"

"What's this 'we' stuff?" Brian said. "I didn't do anything. You threw the tomato, remember? And besides, I catch the bus tomorrow at noon."

I couldn't believe what I was hearing. Among my friends, it was all for one and one for all. No one ratted on anyone else; we didn't leave anyone behind, and above all, we went to the gallows together. But here was my own cousin—flesh and blood—bailing out on me! It was at that moment, after years of following him blindly, that I realized Brian was a snake.

The next day I was glad to see him go. We took him to the bus stop at 11:30, and my mom and dad bought him some comic books for the trip. I wanted to punch him goodbye, but instead I shook his hand. "You're a jerk," I whispered through clenched teeth.

"I hope you get in lots of trouble," Brian replied and stepped onto the bus.

At lunch, it seemed as if Brian was about to get his wish. "Son," my mother said, "Mr. Hamlett called this morning. He asked if you would come over to the hotel sometime today." I almost choked. "He has a little work he wants you to help him with."

"Mr. Hamlett is a fine man," my father said. "I appreciate him coming up with jobs for you now and then. Work will keep a boy out of mischief." Then he said to my mother, "What's he needing done?"

"Painting the porch or something," Mom answered.

"That's odd," my father said, "Bill painted that porch yesterday."

"Seems somebody messed it up last night," she said. "In any case, Andy, you go on over there to help after you finish your sandwich."

During this exchange, I scarcely breathed. Did they know? Had Brian told them? Maybe they knew because they were parents and they could read my mind. Why were they torturing me? Are they waiting for me to confess? Can they hear my heart beating through the silence? "Yes, ma'am," I said.

Mr. Hamlett was standing on the front porch with paint and a brush when I arrived. It was as if someone had told him I was on my way. "Hey, Andy," he said, smiling. "Thanks for coming over." I grinned weakly.

"Take a look at this. Mrs. Hamlett and I painted this porch yesterday, and last night somebody threw a tomato on it before it was dry. Can you clean this up, sand it off, and paint it again?"

"Yes, sir," I answered.

"Great," he said. "Thanks for the help. Mrs. Hamlett was really hurt that someone would do this to us, so I'd like to go ahead and get it out of the way." With that, he turned to go inside.

"Mr. Hamlett," I said in a whisper.

He stopped, turned around, and peered over his glasses at me. "Yes?"

"Can I mow your lawn, too?" I asked.

He put his hands on my shoulders, looked directly into my eyes and said, "Now why would you want to do that?"

I told him everything. I told him how we had sneaked out of the house, how I had stolen a tomato from the Carper's garden, and how I had thrown it on his porch. I told him how sorry I was and how I hadn't meant to hurt Mrs. Hamlett's feelings. I may have even cried a little.

Mr. Hamlett shook my hand and said it was all forgiven. He said that he appreciated me being a man about it and owning up to my mistakes. I repainted the porch, mowed, and got home in time for supper. My dad was waiting by the garage.

"You look tired," he said. "Clean up and go on inside. Mom has soup on the table. Tomato, I think it is. By the way, Rick Carper called while you were out. He has some work he needs done tomorrow in his garden."

We aren't sure where he goes during his long absences or where he stays when he's in town, but one thing is certain—people love Monk Myers.

# Monk's Back in Town

**M**onk Myers was in town last week. That just about says it all. I won't be rambling around this month like I usually do—hopping from one bit of news to the next, trying to find something interesting to fill the space of this column. When the first person I contacted told me that Monk had arrived for a visit, I knew I had a story.

Never mind the city council fight over garbage pickup or the petting zoo in the parking lot of Norman's Groceteria. Never mind that Meg Reed was knocked down by a llama who licked her face, scaring the child almost to death. Forget that Halloween is coming and the wealth of material that provides. Monk Myers was in town this week. Any other news pales by comparison.

Glenda Perkins told me, "He came walking down College Avenue about 10:00 last Tuesday morning. He spoke to everybody like he sees us every day, but it's been at least a year since he's been around."

Monk Myers may or may not be from Sawyerton Springs. He is by all accounts well over 100 years old, and he has been wandering in and out of town for as long as anyone can remember. Bill Hamlett, who is in his fifties, says that when he was a boy, Monk already looked like he was about to fall over and die. The only thing anyone knows for sure is that Monk is somehow related to Miss Luna Myers.

Miss Luna is 83 and has watched Monk come and go longer than the rest of us. "He is not irresponsible," she says, "but I have never known him to have a job, a car, or a house. He somehow seems to be around when people need him, yet he never needs anything himself . . . and he was already old when I was a girl!"

Monk looks like a bum. He is short and skinny with a long, white beard. His clothes are old, but clean, and he is always wearing tennis shoes. He carries a suitcase wherever he goes, but no one has ever seen him open it.

We aren't sure where he goes during his long absences or where he stays when he's in town, but one thing is certain—people love Monk Myers. They love to hear him talk. He is a witty old man, and he is as wise as his years might suggest. He knows everyone's face and has a memory for dates and details. Names are his only problem.

"Whatcha been doing lately, Monk?" Kevin Perkins asked as they passed in front of the post office.

"Ain't been watchin' TV, Calvin, that's fer blame sure," Monk answered. "It ain't the same since Andy Griffin was doing his thing. And I'm not too crazy about some of them preacher shows—you'd think you's watchin' the International Church of Pancakes and Discount House of Worship."

Kevin laughed as he related the exchange to Glenda later that evening. They recalled that Monk never seemed to have any use for organized religion. The one time anyone had ever seen him in church, years ago, he told Pastor Ward that his sermon had been really good that morning. "Yep," Monk said. "It must've been. You interrupted my thoughts three or four times."

Monk also does not like politicians. "The truth shall set you free," he said. "That's why so many of them fellers is in jail."

Over lunch at Norman's, Monk enthralled more than 20 people. "It's like this here, Benny Paul," he said to Billy Pat, "I ain't voted for nobody since Franklin Delaware Roosevelt. He messed things up so bad that nothing works anymore. This Bill Clifton guy—I coulda told ya he wadn't gonna make it—he's too purty. Just remember Psalm 108, Verse 9: 'Let his days be few; let another take his office.' "

Monk talked for awhile about welfare, the arms race ("The one that's got the arms wins the race"), and Ted Kennedy. "Now there was an ugly kid. Nothing against him, understand. I'm sure he was bright and sociable. But he was ugly. He's kinda fat now. Have you seen him lately? Sweats a lot, too. Smart man, I'm sure, but he was an ugly kid. If you'd a shaved his head and stuck a banjo in his hands, he'd a looked like that boy from *Deliverance*."

By the time Monk ambled out the door, the lunch crowd had grown to at least 50 people. They almost followed him down the street, so anxious were they to catch everything he said. "You'll see, Tim, Dave, you too, Mick," he said to Tom, Dick, and Max. "Nothing comes from politics. Remember, *poli* means 'many' and *tics* means 'bloodsuckers.' "

One might think that Monk is an old grouch. Old, yes, but not a grouch. He is gentle and thought provoking in a slightly sarcastic sort of way. Monk is seen as a philosopher. People listen because he seems to be able to help them with any problem.

"If not you, who? If not now, when?" Monk posed that question to Kevin several years ago while Kevin was contemplating using his construction company to build an extension on the library. Kevin built the extension, felt good about the work he'd done, and got several other jobs as a result.

Monk has very little patience with what he considers ungrateful people. Once, he told Miss Edna Thigpen to "wake up, get a life, and be happy. If you aren't happy where you are, it's a dead cinch you won't be happy where you ain't!" Then he smiled and said,

"Besides, you're too good looking to waste that face on a frown."
Miss Edna has smiled ever since.

Something like that happens every time Monk hits town. There is always someone who is changed for the better; someone who is guided to the answer to a problem.

Just yesterday, Monk sat on the bench outside of Norman's. It wasn't long before Jerry Anderson wandered up. "Hi Monk," Jerry said. "You busy?"

"Busy waitin' on you," Monk said and grinned. "Take a load off."

When Jerry sat down, Monk said, "You got trouble don't you, Harry." Monk made the statement as a fact, not a question.

"Yessir. Is it that obvious?"

"Well," Monk said shrugging, "most young fellers are at work this time of day. Most of 'em ain't out lookin' for an old goober like me to talk to."

Jerry frowned. "A guy I know said you might be able to help me."

"I might could see it from a different angle, that's all."

"Okay," Jerry took a deep breath, "Here goes. I hope this doesn't shock you, but I'm having marital problems."

"I already knew that, son," Monk said.

Jerry's mouth dropped open. "How did you know?" he asked.

"Simple," Monk replied, "you're married. If you're married, you're gonna have marital problems. It's part of the deal."

Jerry stared at Monk for a long moment and said, "Monk, we're worried, maybe our marriage was a mistake. We're so . . . different."

Monk laughed out loud and slapped Jerry on the shoulder. Then he looked into Jerry's eyes and said, "Son, if you were both alike, one of you would be unnecessary." With that, Monk got up and walked away.

"Wait," Jerry said as he caught up with the old man. "I'm not sure you understand. This is very hard."

Monk's smile faded, but his eyes remained soft. "Yep, I understand," he said. "I understand that nothin' worthwhile is easy. Now take your marriage, for instance. It's worthwhile, but it'll

# Monk's Back in Town

never be easy." Glancing at his pocket watch, Monk continued. "My time is almost up here, but I want you to remember one thing: Facts are the enemy of truth. Don Quixote said that first, but I've used it more than he did. Another way of saying the same thing is that if what you want is important enough, the facts don't matter." Monk turned again to go.

Desperately, Jerry grabbed the old man's arm and said, "Please, don't go yet, I don't understand."

Monk turned once again and said, "The facts are that your wife squeezes the toothpaste in the middle of the tube. She's never cooked your eggs the way you like 'em. She likes sad movies, she doesn't enjoy fishing, and she'll never understand your jokes. And yes, she did call you a jerk this morning. Those, son, are the facts. But the truth is that you love her and she loves you. Now, if you can keep your eye on the truth, are the facts really that important?"

At that moment, Jerry couldn't tell if Monk had slipped into the bushes beside Norman's or if he had walked around the corner. Jerry's eyes were filled with tears, and it seemed to him that Monk had simply disappeared.

That was yesterday. No one has seen Monk in town since. Most everyone figures he'll be back, but a few are not so sure. For the first time ever, the old man left his suitcase. After some discussion, it was opened by Kevin Perkins, Pastor Ward, and Miss Luna Myers.

In the suitcase they found several packages of assorted seeds and a note that read: "Time is of the essence. I am now in another town. Sawyerton Springs was never my only concern, nor should it be yours. Your lives are showing the evidence of laughter, hope, encouragement, love, and understanding. But with life's fruit comes a responsibility, for there is more to our existence than to be mere gatherers of this fruit. We must also plant seeds for those who follow. These special seeds are for you. I'm expecting great things, and I'll see you again. —Monk."

"Please," I said, "stay away." I jerked a
mirror up off the table and brandished
it like a weapon.

# Dentist the Menace

C abell Outlaw was cleaning out his files in the back room of his gas station last week. In an old cigar box, he found a ticket for a suit his father had left to be altered at Martin's Department Store in Foley. The ticket was dated May 22, 1959—more than 35 years ago.

The ticket had not been stamped, signifying receipt, so Cabell assumed that his father had simply forgotten to pick up the suit. Cabell grinned.

He was still grinning later that day as he presented the ticket to Mike Martin in the men's department. "Need to pick up this suit, Mike," Cabell said. "We were having the cuffs and sleeves let out."

Mike took the ticket, glanced at it, and went behind the counter. After only a few minutes of poking through files of his own, Mike produced a piece of paper, stared at it a moment, and said, "Cabell, those alterations won't be ready until next Thursday."

The people of Sawyerton Springs have shopped in Martin's Department Store since 1931. Located in Foley, it was started during the Depression by Mickey Martin, and it has remained a family business all these years. After Mickey's death in 1969, his son and daughter-in-law, Mike and Melanie, kept the place going.

Martin's is by far the biggest building in Foley. It is a three-story, red-brick structure that takes up most of a city block. Huge windows surround the first floor, and Melanie keeps them filled with the latest fashions from Birmingham and Memphis.

September is a busy month at Martin's. The "Back to School Sale" is in progress, and the outdoor department picks up with the advent of hunting season.

Most children from the Springs only visit the department store three times a year—once for school clothes, once for summer clothes, and once at Christmas to see the "Santa's Workshop" window exhibit.

The Christmas visit was the only one I ever enjoyed because it was the only one for which I was not required to try on clothes. I hated shopping with my mother. As if the 42-mile drive to Foley wasn't bad enough, it always took us at least an hour to get through "Housewares" and "Home Furnishings" on the first floor and "Ladies Wear" and "Shoes" on the second floor before we ever saw "Boys" on the third.

Melanie was a friend of my mother's, so she usually waited on us in the boy's department. I stood around while she and my mother made small talk, then they picked out what they wanted me to wear, which, of course, was the same every six months—two pairs of jeans, one pair of dress pants, five shirts, four pairs of socks, a pair of dress shoes, and a pair of sneakers.

As I tried them on, looking somewhat newer, but more or less the same as I did six months earlier, Melanie would point at me and say, "Fabulous. Fabulous! You just look precious!" My mother would smile and say things like, "He's growing like a weed," or "Can you believe the size of his feet? He's a 10½ right now, and he's only in the fifth grade. He's going to be a big man." Melanie would point at her and say, "That's exactly right!"

# Dentist the Menace

The other reason I hated going to Foley was Dr. Nealis, our dentist. Since Foley was so far, my mother always killed two birds with one stone and scheduled my six-month checkup on the same day we went for clothes. As badly as I hated shopping, nothing compared with my dislike for the dentist.

It wasn't that Dr. Nealis wasn't an okay guy, it was just that dentists scared me to death. It also never helped my attitude that all the adults in town referred to him in less than glowing terms. "Bloody Jim" was one I heard more than once. I was too young to realize that their animosity toward Dr. Nealis had nothing to do with his dental ability—he had hurt their feelings.

Our town has never had its own dentist. Therefore, when Jim Nealis, who was born and reared in Sawyerton Springs, finished dental school at the University of Alabama–Birmingham, everyone assumed that he would open an office in his own hometown. He didn't, and they never forgave him.

Dr. Rudolph Posey, who had been the dentist in Foley for 45 years, retired and sold his practice to Jim, building and all. "For gosh sakes," people said, "we have a mortician here, but no dentist!"

Max the mortician agreed. "You're right," he said. "It's a crazy thing. I see a lot of mouths that've been dead longer than their owners." I, for one, did not want a dead mouth, but that is the only reason I crawled into that dentist chair every six months.

When Dr. Nealis entered the examining room on the day I am about to describe, he was smiling. Dr. Nealis was always smiling, which, I thought, was a good thing for a dentist to do—it kind of showed me that the man could at least take care of his own teeth. He was about 5' 10", in his mid-thirties, and prematurely gray, probably as a result of treating patients like me.

"Hey, buddy," he said, even though I did not feel like his buddy, "You been eating lots of candy? I need the business, you know!" This was Dr. Nealis' idea of a joke, and I heard it every time I saw him.

"Ha, ha, ha," I laughed nervously, "Do I have any cavities?"

"Well," he said, "let me look in your mouth. That's the easiest way for me to tell, you know."

"I know," I said.

Sitting down beside me, he grabbed what looked like a curved ice pick, and then he said, " 'Course, you don't have to open your mouth. I could go in through your nose."

I opened my mouth as wide as I could. My nose, like my feet, was proportionately larger than the rest of me, and I wasn't sure if he was kidding or not.

As he pushed and pulled on my teeth, he quietly talked to Arlene, his wife and assistant, who made notes on a pad. "We're missing a molar," he told her, "and I think we're gonna be missing another one. This joker will have to be extracted." She made a note.

I was concerned. Extract was not a word with which I was familiar. Although he had both hands and an ice pick in my mouth, I said, "Whmahstakmen?"

"I'm sorry," he said as he placed the ice pick on a table. "Did I hurt you?"

"No," I said. "What does extract mean?"

"It means that we have to make room for one of your permanent teeth."

"So what's extract mean," I asked again.

"Pull. Extract means pull. We have to . . . ."

I was already out of the chair. Unfortunately, I was so scared that I had gotten out on the wrong side. Dr. Nealis and his wife were now blocking the door. "No," I said as I backed into the corner. "No. No. No!"

Lee Peyton had told me about having his tooth pulled only a month before, and it had sounded horrible. Dr. Nealis had used the claw of a hammer to hold down Lee's bottom jaw. Then, with another hammer, he had cracked the tooth with several swings and pulled out the pieces with a pair of pliers. There had been blood everywhere, but Lee had never cried. He swore it had happened just like that, and now Bloody Jim was after me.

I was only a kid, but this was not going to happen. "Please," I said, "stay away." I jerked a mirror up off the table and brandished it like a weapon. I had seen the ice pick right beside it, but even in a state of panic, I knew that my dad would whip me for holding an ice pick on the only dentist in the county.

"Hey, buddy," Dr. Nealis said soothingly, "don't worry. This is not going to hurt at all. Honest. You won't feel a thing."

"Really?" I asked. My bottom lip was quivering, and I desperately wanted to believe him. At that point, I almost put down the mirror. Maybe Lee had been lying. Maybe it wouldn't be so bad after all. "You promise I won't feel anything?"

"I promise you won't feel anything," he said. I relaxed for a moment, but then he made a mistake. He added, "You won't feel anything, because first we're going to knock you out!"

That did it. I yelled as loud as I could: "Ahhhhhh! Stay away!"

My God! The man was going to hit me in the head with the hammer before he ever started on me—and with my own mother in the waiting room. "Ahhhhhh!" I yelled again. "Stay away!"

Quickly, I lunged for the automatic water gun (still not wanting to risk the ice pick) and sprayed Dr. Nealis right in the face. This was an act that my mother personally witnessed, the commotion having drawn her into the battle. It was not her fight, and she should not have tried to take part, but she did, so I sprayed her, too—an act I immediately recognized as an error on my part.

At that point, I was left alone in the corner with my water gun and mirror. About 15 minutes later, the end of this story walked into the room in the form of my father. He had been located in the lawn and garden department of Martin's, and he did not seem very happy.

He looked at me for a moment as if I had lost my mind, which indeed for a while there, I had. Then, he pointed at me and said that if I sprayed him I would get a whipping right in front of everybody and that he did not mean maybe. He practically slam-dunked me into the chair, put a mask on my face, punched a button, and left. "Breathe" was the last thing he said.

The next thing I knew, we were in the car driving home. My jaw felt numb, but I didn't remember anything. The extraction had actually been painless.

Another good point was that while I had been in Dr. Nealis' chair, my mother had done all the shopping. I had two pairs of jeans, one pair of dress pants, five shirts, four pairs of socks, a pair of dress shoes, and a pair of sneakers. That part of my day had been painless, too.

"We have more than we need," he said to the group gathered around his truck. "I hope you can use them."

# Church Gangs and Other Hot Items

A fter calling several friends in and around town the past couple of weeks, I have come to the frightening conclusion that nothing of any note has occurred. This, of course, puts me in the awkward position of confessing to you, the reader, that I have nothing about which to write!

It was bound to happen sooner or later . . . nothing, I mean. That is the risk a correspondent takes when he or she (and in this case me) ties himself to a particular location. Especially if that location happens to be Sawyerton Springs.

I must admit that I was tempted to simply "make something up" like real authors do, but since I am a correspondent—not an author—and you have come to expect the truth, anything less would be unfair. Besides, it would be too easy for you to catch me.

# Church Gangs and Other Hot Items

My challenge is in relating anything of interest with the information I received this month from my regular sources. It's tough to put several thousand words on paper based on the news "it is hot." Seven people gave that same answer to my question about what was happening in town.

Actually, the heat is probably part of the reason I wasn't able to get a complete story from anyone. The people in Sawyerton Springs are generally a good natured bunch, and I think they put up with my invasion of their privacy quite well, but when temperatures exceed one hundred degrees for days on end, even they can be testy.

"Hot enough for you?" That's all I said to Miss Edna Thigpen yesterday afternoon when I got her on the phone. "No, Andy," she said, "I'd like to crank it up another hundred degrees so that my blood actually starts to boil!" (Whew! Sorry I asked, Miss Edna. I'll touch base with you next month!)

Heat does that to people. Especially to the kind of people who don't believe in air conditioning. A prevailing opinion among some of the older residents seems to be, "My father got along without it, and it ain't no hotter now than it was then!" To them, a window unit is a visible sign of weakness.

It is fortunate then, I suppose, that most people in town do have air conditioning. As hot as it gets there, it would be a grouchy place without it.

As it is, tempers flared at the town council meeting last week. Kevin Perkins and Jeff Deas almost got into it over the curfew controversy. "It was a dumb idea to begin with," Kevin said, "and three days of it is enough!"

Jeff, the town's only volunteer policeman, had instituted a curfew for kids younger than 18. He blew the fire whistle at 10:00 sharp. This was done with the blessings of a town worried sick about their children—and all because of an article in the newspaper. Miss Luna Myers had written a piece in the *Sentinel* entitled: WILL YOUR BOY BE A CRIP OR A BLOOD? The subhead was "Gang

Activity . . . Is It Headed Our Way?"

The immediate impact that the article had was to make the town suspicious of its youth. Tom Henley, the owner of Henley's Hardware, refused to sell spray paint to Todd Rollins. "If your father really wants this to paint a porch swing," Tom told him, "he'll be more than happy to pick it up himself."

When Dick arrived at the store, Tom said, "I'm sorry, but that article said red was a gang color, and I didn't figure you'd want to take chances with the life of your boy." Dick understood.

Quickly, the young people were on probation. Was the youth choir from the Methodist church really taking rocks out of the church yard to keep them from hitting the lawn mower, or were they collecting them to throw through someone's window? Who knew?

The curfew was in place before most people had discussed it, but soon, cooler heads prevailed, and it was removed. The children in this town had never really done anything bad before, so what were they all upset about? "And besides," Kevin said before he sat down, "when the whistle blows at ten, it's waking everybody up!"

After telling me that it was hot, Liz Reed told me that everything was going well at Vacation Bible School. She, Rebecca Peyton, and Glenda Perkins were teaching the first, second, and third graders this year at Grace Fellowship Baptist Church.

For a week (in air conditioning) the ladies showed the children how to build churches out of Play-Dough and pot holders out of Popsicle sticks. They taught them songs like "Deep and Wide," "The B-I-B-L-E, Yes That's the Book for Me," and "If You're Happy and You Know It Clap Your Hands [clap, clap]."

Having been raised in a Catholic home, Liz had not been aware until recently of all the variations on that particular song. There was "If You're Happy and You Know It Stomp Your Feet [stomp, stomp]," "If You're Happy and You Know It Say Amen [a-men]," and, of course, the ever popular "If You're Happy and You Know

It Do All Three [clap, clap; stomp, stomp; a-men]."

Liz enjoyed story time most of all. It was a chance to listen to the children's comments about different Bible characters. On Thursday, she watched Glenda and Rebecca skillfully act out the story of David and Goliath, after which Liz asked the second graders if anyone knew the moral of that story. One of the boys did. "Duck," he said.

Liz also enjoys watching her own daughter, Meg, interact with the other first graders. Meg is an intelligent, self-assured, little girl who is the spitting image of her mother—same hairstyle, same bright smile. She also has the same quick mind of her parents.

Last year, her father, Max, inadvertently backed the car over the family dog. All the rest of that day, he and Liz agonized over how to explain to Meg what had happened. "Honey," they finally told her, "Prince has gone to be with God."

Meg had one question. "Well," she wanted to know, "what does God want with a dead dog?"

"I'm sorry," Norman Green said when I called. "There's really nothing going on. I hate you haven't got anything to write about. I'd go do something crazy myself if it weren't so dang hot."

Norman has been working in his garden at night to escape the heat. With a flashlight, he bends over and pulls weeds from around his tomatoes. This year, Norman planted corn, peas, butter beans, cucumbers, okra, yellow squash, bell peppers, zucchini, and tomatoes. So did everyone else in town.

Growing up as I did in Sawyerton Springs, I thought for a while that it was actually a law that one had to have a garden. It was sort of strange now that I think of it. We all planted the same things, we admired them in each other's backyards, then we gave it all to each other!

Every Sunday, the coat room at church looked like a roadside vegetable stand. Sacks of tomatoes, corn, cucumbers, and zucchini—especially zucchini. "We had more than we needed," my father would say to Mr. Rawls as he handed over a grocery sack full of the green squash. "Hope you can use them!"

Mr. Rawls would smile and say how they certainly could as he admired the color, texture, and firmness of what he said was his favorite vegetable. Then he would give us a bag of tomatoes and okra, which, believe it or not, just happened to be my dad's favorite!

Although the following week my father might give okra and tomatoes to the Rawls and get zucchini in return, no one ever tired of this tradition. We gave each other so much that, by the time I turned 18, I doubted whether I had ever eaten anything from our own garden.

We all enjoyed an ample amount of whatever we planted with one glaring exception. Watermelons. No one had any luck growing watermelons. Even though we tried year after year, there seemed to be something about the soil in our area that precluded growing watermelons.

As a community, we wanted to quit trying to force these melons to grow where they obviously did not want to, and every year we determined to do just that—quit. But every year, the *Sentinel* would run a picture of someone from Foley or Dothan or somewhere else close by, and they would be holding a watermelon that weighed a thousand pounds.

I cannot exaggerate the impact those pictures had on our town. "Look at this," someone would say. "I don't believe it! Why, it says right here that the man just threw some seeds out his kitchen window and got this monster for his efforts. Heck, this didn't happen 40 miles from here. If this goober can do this by accident, I know I can grow one. Look at the guy. He doesn't look like he has the sense to come in out of the rain!" Soon, the whole town would be planting watermelons again.

Summer after summer this went on until one year, Haywood Perkins (Kevin's father) hit pay dirt. His garden was in a secluded area behind their house. Consequently, no one ever got a really good look at how things were coming along. Around town, word from Haywood was that he "might just have something this year in the watermelon department."

I'll always remember the look on the faces of the people at church that Sunday morning in July when Mr. Perkins drove up in a pickup truck loaded down with huge watermelons. "We had more than we needed," he said to the group gathered around his truck. "I hope you can use them." Then he walked inside.

Mr. Perkins never professed any great knowledge or secret formula. Neither had he sold his soul to the watermelon devil. He seemed to be as perplexed as everyone else . . . until the following year.

A man in a truck full of watermelons pulled up in front of Henley's Hardware one day about lunchtime. Several of the town's businessmen were standing out on the curb. "Excuse me," he said, "I came through here last year selling melons and found a guy who bought my whole load. I don't know his name, but I'd sure like to find him again." The men just looked at each other. The jig was up.

I'm quite sure that right now in Sawyerton Springs, as hot as it is, there is a boy working in his father's garden. I say his father's garden because it will never be his garden until he has a boy of his own who is old enough to work in it.

As a teenager, I dug the soil, planted the seeds, pulled the weeds, and watered the plants. When my father had friends over, he would invite them to take a look at *his* garden! Amazingly enough, the year I moved away from home, Dad decided that he was getting too old to have a garden. He was 44 at the time.

As I close this month's chronicle of my hometown's activities, it occurs to me that maybe I did have something to write about after all. I'm certain that it was not as thrilling as it would have been had I made it up, but I suppose that's the magic of this place . . . that it is not thrilling.

It is a place where the paper comes out once a week and

everyone already knows what's in it. When the pastor speaks on Sunday morning, his congregation already knows what he will say. As the children bring home their report cards, the parents already know their grades. This is a place of memories. Good memories.

As you read these stories in the future, please remember that if something unusual is happening in town, I will tell you. But if it is only hot, I will tell you that, too. That is the risk a correspondent takes when he or she (and in this case me) ties himself to a particular location. Especially if that location happens to be Sawyerton Springs.

For booking information, additional copies of this book,
Andy's earlier books, *Storms of Perfection*,
Volumes I and II, or to see other
popular items by Andy Andrews such as comedy
cassettes, motivational tapes, and a variety of T-shirts,
please call for a free color brochure:

**(800) 726-ANDY**
24 hours a day

or, you may write to:

**Andy Andrews**
P.O. Box 17321
Nashville, TN 37217
USA